"Sorry, Mollie. I shou
questioning you."

"Why not? You're their *daed* ⌐ ▢
to know what they're learning and how. I encourage parents to ask questions. Doing that avoids misunderstandings when what the scholars repeat to their parents isn't close to what I meant for them to share."

A faint smile tipped his lips. "I get the message. Don't assume."

She glanced over her shoulder at a burst of laughter from inside. "I need to go."

"I understand. I've got meetings today, and I'm late for the first one." He grimaced. "The day didn't start off well because Sam didn't want to leave the house."

"He was scared of coming to school?"

"I think he's too tired."

Sympathy cut through the guardrails she'd put in place around her heart, and she knew she had to keep everything between them professional.

Another swell of laughter, louder this time, made her cut him off with a wave before she hurried inside and shut the door. She knew, as her ears strained for the sound of the wagon heading to the road, that concentrating on the scholars was going to be more difficult than she'd expected when she'd invited Noah to drop off his *kinder*.

Much more difficult.

Jo Ann Brown loves stories with happily-ever-after endings. A former military officer, she is thrilled to write about finding that forever love all over again with her characters. She and her husband (her real hero who knows how to fix computer problems quickly when she's on deadline) divide their time between Western Massachusetts and Amish country in Pennsylvania. She loves hearing from readers, so drop her a note at joannbrownbooks.com.

HEALING HER AMISH HEART

JO ANN BROWN

LOVE INSPIRED
INSPIRATIONAL ROMANCE

LOVE INSPIRED®
INSPIRATIONAL ROMANCE

Recycling programs
for this product may
not exist in your area.

ISBN-13: 978-1-335-93694-3

Healing Her Amish Heart

Copyright © 2024 by Jo Ann Ferguson

Love Inspired
22 Adelaide St. West, 41st Floor
Toronto, Ontario M5H 4E3, Canada
www.LoveInspired.com

Printed in Lithuania

MIX
Paper | Supporting
responsible forestry
FSC® C021394

He hath made every thing beautiful in his time:
also he hath set the world in their heart,
so that no man can find out the work
that God maketh from the beginning to the end.
—*Ecclesiastes* 3:11

For Frankie

You've helped make our house a beautiful home—thanks!

Chapter One

It was nothing like he'd imagined.

Noah Frye glanced from his sleeping *kinder* on the van seat beside him to the vast expanse beyond his window where he sat behind the driver. When he'd been invited to Lost River, Colorado, he'd envisioned huge mountains topped with snow. In the San Luis Valley in the south-central part of the state, the land was flat. Though mountains highlighted the horizon in every direction, the road was so straight it could have been drawn with a ruler.

What an alien vista!

He took in Colorado's many unique colors. Would he be able to use them in his work? How would he make them look as beautiful as the ones God had created?

He couldn't. The moment he started comparing his work to God's splendor would be when he turned his back on Him. His fingers, woven together on his lap, tightened as he wondered why God had turned His back on *him*.

"Are we there yet?"

Noah's six-year-old daughter's question wasn't unexpected. Either Angela or her five-year-old brother, Sam, had been asking it every mile during their journey from Wisconsin. Hints of chocolate clung to their cheeks, though they'd had the candy bars before they got off the train. Their clothes looked as rumpled as if they'd slept in them. Which they had. He tried not to think of what their *mamm* would have said if she'd seen them in such a state.

He must appear to be in equally sad shape. His clothes were splattered with paint. If he'd had a chance to do laundry before they'd left Wisconsin, he wouldn't look like he'd cleaned his brushes on his trousers.

During each step of his journey, Noah had asked himself if he was doing the right thing taking his *kinder* with him. Yet he couldn't leave them behind. They were all he had after a fire in Lancaster County that had left him a widower.

If I'd been home...

Those words had been echoing through his mind for five years.

"Daed!" A small hand tugged on his coat. "Is this *there*?"

Noah had been so lost in thought he hadn't noticed the van had stopped in front of a low-slung cottage with a broad porch. Stunted bushes edged the house. A cottonwood tree shaded the house's southern side. Two barns were farther from the road. One was metal—rusty metal—and looked as if a strong breath would make it collapse. The other, painted a dull cream, was twice the length of the house. A wide door was open on one side, and he saw stalls inside. Was it a stable?

"Ja, Sam," he replied to his son, who was straining to see around his sister. "This is where we're going."

The *kinder* cheered, but he heard their fatigue. He hoped the Marquezes, their hosts in San Luis Valley, would understand the two hadn't slept much in the past three days.

Noah unhooked his seat belt while dust from the road swirled around the van.

Grinning, Angela grabbed her brother's arm as hair bounced around her face. The fine red strands refused to remain in its netting. "We're here, Sam!"

"Where's here?" asked Sam, the practical one.

"Where we're going!" Angela shook hair out of her eyes.

Every day, Noah saw more of his late wife in Angela's face. Her greenish-gray eyes and those soft red curls. Nobody would doubt Sam was his son because they had the same dark brown eyes and black hair. His heart swelled with love for his *kinder*, who had kept him from surrendering to grief after Betty Jane's death.

I'll take care of them until my last breath, he'd whispered as his wife's coffin was lowered into the ground.

While the driver got out and went to get their luggage, Noah grabbed his straw hat and Sam's. The *kinder* unhooked themselves from their booster seats and edged around the plywood box where he kept his painting supplies. He motioned for the kids to get out. They did, eager to explore their home for the next three months.

Guilt twinged as he thought about uprooting the *kinder* again, but Angela and Sam grinned when they grabbed their backpacks and roller suitcases. Noah took the handle of the box on wheels.

After Noah had thanked the *Englisch* driver, the van pulled away. Noah opened a gate in a picket fence and led the way to the porch. Petunias grew in clay pots set on either side of the door, adding color to the otherwise drab gray floor and dusty white clapboards.

He knocked on the dark green door. Glancing at the kids, he watched them trying to quell their yawns.

The door didn't open, so he knocked again. The Marquezes had assured him they'd be here.

"Are we living on the porch?" asked Sam.

"No." Noah hoped he sounded reassuring.

The Marquezes were *Englischers*, and Noah had assumed they'd want him to use the front door. He raised his hand to knock a third time, but the door opened. Shock short-circuited his *gut* sense when he saw the woman who had one hand on the jamb. The lapis-lazuli-blue eyes in her delicate face were wide as they met his gaze. A slender nose had a sprinkling of freckles on the left side, but on the right side three scars looked as if a giant cat had clawed her. Her mouth was curving its way into a smile, but it froze as, after seeing the conical *kapp* covering her golden blond hair, he asked, "Who are you?"

"I'm Mollie—"

Sam peeked around Noah and blurted, "What happened to your face?"

Mollie Lehman watched the broad-shouldered man's face grow pale, then flush. He was embarrassed by the *kind*'s question, but she was accustomed to youngsters' blunt questions. In fact, she preferred them to the surreptitious looks adults believed she wouldn't see. Though the car-and-buggy collision had been six years ago, her face reminded her of it every time her eyes caught her reflection.

Leaning forward as if talking to her youngest scholar, she said, "I got hurt, and God sent me healing. Can you see where His fingers touched me?"

The little boy's eyes widened, and he nodded after glancing at the girl beside him. Both wore drooping backpacks. The boy, who appeared to be five or six, was a miniature of the man, though his face had a soft pudginess about it. The little girl must resemble her *mamm* because her ginger hair fell in front of greenish-gray eyes. The two appeared close in age and looked exhausted.

As the man did, she realized when she straightened. Gray arcs clung beneath his dark eyes. She could understand fatigue. She'd spent the last hour working on her letter to *The*

Budget for this week. For over two years, since the previous scribe had moved away, she'd served her church district. She loved the chance to share the local news—both *gut* and sad—with plain subscribers around the world.

It wasn't easy to find time to write during the last weeks of school. The *kinder* were working extra hard to memorize their verses and songs for their end-of-the-year presentation. It'd been impossible today for them to sit still. She'd spent an hour with them outdoors, letting them play ball and work off excess energy.

She loved the scholars. At school, they were her *kinder*. The only *kinder* she would ever have, according to the *doktor* who'd treated her after the accident. Being with them was a joy, but every day, they went home. She was left alone. That gave her time to think.

Too much time.

While the scholars were excited about the school year's end, she dreaded it. She hadn't found a summer job. She'd been looking, but nothing had materialized. The extra money she could earn would help pay the last of *Daed*'s medical bills. The community had helped with the biggest ones for the hospital. *Mamm* had insisted the family couldn't ask for more help, though they might have to sell some of their hundred acres if they didn't find another way to cover those bills for *Daed*'s losing battle with cancer, as well as Mollie's after the buggy accident.

An accident she couldn't remember. Nobody spoke of it to her. Though she'd made discreet queries, everyone acted as if it had never happened. Who else had been there that night? Why had *she* been there? Why wouldn't anyone talk to her about it?

She needed to remember God must have had a reason for changing the path of her life in one split second. She could have died. The *doktors* and the nurses had told her that, believing she'd be so relieved to be alive she'd forget what she'd lost.

"I'm Mollie Lehman," she repeated when the man in the doorway didn't say anything. The hair beneath his straw hat was the color of the night's shadows, while his eyes were the darkest brown she'd ever seen. The angles of his face looked as rough and unfinished as the peaks of the Sangre de Cristo Mountains that rose along the east side of the valley. His beard couldn't hide the sharp edge of his jaw. He wore plain clothes covered with splotches of red, yellow and blue paint. "Who are you?"

He looked past her, and she was aware her brother Kolton had left one of his shoes in the middle of the living room. Where was the other one? She saw its toe sticking beneath her quilting frame near the stairs. Her other brother, Tyler, had skiing magazines scattered across the sofa.

"I'm Noah. Noah Frye," the man said, his voice as deep and rumbling as summer thunder over the mountains.

That didn't tell her anything, but Mollie said, "*Komm* in." She opened the door as far as it could go and motioned for the trio to enter. "You must be tired after your long trip."

The man frowned. "Why would you assume we're traveling?"

"Your luggage." She gestured toward the bags and a large wooden box behind them on the porch.

He sighed and rubbed a hand across his forehead. "Sorry. Tired. My brain needs about a week's sleep."

"Bring your luggage inside. Dust gets into everything around here."

He grabbed the handles on the biggest suitcase, motioning for the *kinder* to enter before him. They dragged identical black suitcases on wheels. "These two are my daughter and son. Angela and Sam."

"I'm six," Angela announced. "He's my little brother. He's five."

"I've got big brothers. Two of them," Mollie said, pleased. *Kinder* were more accepting of differences than adults. Another reason she liked spending time with them.

She smiled as their *daed* returned to the porch to get the rest of their things. "If I had to guess, I'd say you're Angela." She pointed to the little girl, then the boy. "And you're Sam."

As she'd hoped, the *kinder* giggled.

"If I had to take another guess," she went on, "I'd say you'd like a piece of pie and a big glass of *millich. Mamm* made coconut-custard pie today." She looked past their eager nods to the man who was appraising the living room as he set a backpack and the large wooden box, as tall as his *kinder,* inside the door. It wasn't deep, and she wondered what was in it.

She wanted to ask, but silenced her curiosity when she realized Noah was frowning. What about the simple light green walls and the sofa and pair of rockers, each covered with a quilt, bothered him? Her gaze moved to Kolton's shoes. Noah couldn't be upset at her brother's forgetfulness. Then she realized what was bothering the man and quickly said, "Of course, we need to ask your *daed* if it's okay for you to have a snack this close to supper."

"Please, *Daed,*" the *kinder* said in unison as they shrugged off their backpacks and dropped them on the sofa.

He continued to frown. She should apologize. As a schoolteacher, she knew to check with a parent before suggesting such a treat. Another thought struck her. Where was the *kinder's mamm?*

His scowl eased. "Don't worry about ruining their supper. They can finish a big meal and decide they need something more to eat."

"Growing kids." It was trite, but the best she could do.

"I thought you'd be expecting us."

It was her turn to frown. "Why would you think that?"

"I sent our itinerary ahead of us."

"We never got anything."

"You didn't?" His black eyebrows rose at the same time his shoulders sank as if she'd set Blanca Peak on each one.

She shook her head.

"Daed," the little girl said in a loud whisper. "Pie. Remember?"

"A moment, Angela." He turned to Mollie. "I'm supposed to meet Carlos Marquez. Is he around?"

Everything about why the Fryes had come to her door became clear with his question. "Noah, Carlos and *Doktor* Lynny—"

"His wife is a *doktor*?"

"A veterinarian. They live at 9352 South County Road Four East. This is 9352 South County Road *Three* East. Your driver must have been confused. It happens a lot for folks not familiar with the area."

Noah deflated right in front of her eyes. "How far is the Marquezes' place from here?" Fatigue weighed on every word.

"Less than two miles."

He glanced at the luggage and the youngsters.

Before he could reply, she went on, *"Mamm* is making her afternoon deliveries. When she returns with the buggy, I can take you and your things over to the Marquezes' ranch."

"Danki. When will that be?" He was trying to be gra-

cious, but she could tell he was as eager to leave as his youngsters were to have pie.

Mollie glanced at the clock in the pale yellow kitchen. "Long enough to give you and your youngsters a chance to have a snack and a rest."

The look he gave her this time was filled with appreciation. "I guess pie will be more than welcome if—"

Loud cheers drowned out the rest of his words, and Angela and Sam skipped into the kitchen. They waved, urging the adults to follow.

She sensed Noah's stare as she walked toward the kitchen. When she turned, he averted his eyes. She wanted to tell him not to bother. She'd become accustomed to people gawping when she faced them. It was easy to avoid a mirror, but impossible to escape the shocked expressions aimed at her cheek.

No, she wasn't going to dwell on that. She didn't want to keep the *kinder* waiting. They'd accepted her and her scars.

When she glanced at the table, Mollie almost gasped. She'd left her unfinished letter for *The Budget* there. Snatching the page and the pen from the table before Noah reached it, she shoved them in her pocket. She was being ridiculous. The letter would be read around the world once it was published, but she didn't like anyone to read what she'd written until she was satisfied with it.

The *kinder*'s focus was on the pie on the counter. She hoped their *daed*'s was, too.

Mollie took a deep, steadying breath as Noah sat next to the youngsters at the table with its blue gingham tablecloth. She brought plates and glasses from the cupboards. Noah turned down *kaffi*, saying he wouldn't be able to sleep if he drank a cup.

She kept up a steady monologue while she carried the

pie to the table and cut it. "*Mamm* makes baked goods for two local bakeries as well as the outlet grocery store on County Route Five to the east of us."

"You've got County Routes Three, Four and Five?" Noah asked.

"And one and two west of here." She placed plates in front of the *kinder* and handed each a fork.

"No wonder drivers get lost."

She chuckled and handed him a plate.

The kids began to enjoy their pie after a brief, silent prayer. Mollie remembered she'd offered them *millich*, too.

As she went to the propane fridge, she was surprised when Noah asked, "Do just you and your *mamm* live here?"

She hadn't expected him to continue the conversation. Hunger might have put him into a grim mood. What had she heard her best friend, Ruthanne Geer, call it? Oh, *ja*—hangry. She knew he wasn't trying to discover if she was married. No man, since the accident, had been interested in changing her marital status. They offered friendship. No more. Often, when she was lying alone in the darkness, she told herself she should be grateful to God for the scars on her face. That way, she didn't have to worry about a man being attracted to her until he learned she could never give him a *boppli*.

Pushing aside those thoughts, Mollie drew out the jug of *millich*. "As I told Angela and Sam, I've got two brothers. Tyler and Kolton have taken the farm wagon into Lost River, and *Mamm* has the buggy. Otherwise, I could have taken you over to the Marquezes' right away."

"But we wouldn't have had pie!" exclaimed Sam around a mouthful.

"Sam," drawled his *daed* in a warning tone, "what have we said about talking with your mouth full?"

"Don't?" Bits of pie squirted out of his mouth.

Before Mollie could get a cloth to clean the splatter, the little boy was scooping up each drop with his finger. She smiled as she poured *millich* for her guests.

"I like your pie," Sam said.

"I'm glad to hear that." She smiled. "Because I like you."

"Cool," the little boy said as he jumped from his chair and ran toward the bathroom.

Noah's eyebrows rose at the *Englisch* term. As Angela gave a huge yawn, he said, "They've spent a lot of time around *Englischers*. They know more words in English than I do."

"As long as you keep up with them."

"That's the challenge." He glanced at his pie. To avoid meeting her eyes? "My work has us among *Englischers* rather than the Amish."

"What sort of work do you do?"

"I'm a painter."

Mollie smiled. "You'll find plenty of work around Lost River. The winter cold and the summer heat here aren't kind to paint." She almost said how their barn needed a refreshing, but didn't. There wasn't any money left after they made the payments on the medical bills. Last month, they'd been forced to skip two different debts so they could cover the cost of new fencing for the cattle herd, and they'd received letters with *PAST DUE* stamped in bright red letters on the envelopes. "Once people learn you're here, they'll be eager to get you on a ladder and to work painting houses and barns."

"I'm not that kind of painter." He broke off a flaky bite of crust. "I paint barn quilts."

"Barn quilts? What are those?" She glanced toward her quilt frame in the living room.

"It's not like that quilt," he said as he folded his arms on the table. "A barn quilt is a single quilt square or quilt pattern painted on a large piece of signboard. Each one is hung on a building—usually a barn, which explains the name— in a prominent place, so anyone passing by can enjoy it."

"How big are they?"

"About eight feet by eight feet, though some are half that size." He met her astonished gaze with a grin that transformed his face from daunting to approachable. "I've been painting them in the Midwest."

"You came here to do that?"

"*Ja.* I was contacted by folks in the San Luis Valley to create a quilt trail. Tourists love to travel from one quilt to the next and take photos. At the same time, they stop at shops and restaurants and hotels."

"And brought your *kinder* with you?"

"*Ja.*"

"And their *mamm*?"

That had been the wrong question. She could tell the moment the words popped out of her mouth. His face closed. Her commonplace query had upset him. She couldn't guess why.

Noah knew his reaction to Mollie's question was visible. Hadn't he learned to hide his feelings? The house fire that had destroyed so much of his life had been five years ago. How long was he going to act like a spooked cat each time someone asked a question about his past?

Mollie hadn't asked about the past. She was curious about an Amish man who led such an unusual life, dragging his kids from place to place without a *mamm* to watch over them. Others had asked questions in Ohio and Illinois and Michigan and Indiana and Wisconsin. He'd learned to answer with explanations that didn't mention the tragedy that had altered his life in ways he couldn't have imagined before he saw flames rising through the roof of his home. His tiny *kinder*—Angela had been less than a year old, Sam a newborn—had survived, but his beloved wife, Betty Jane, hadn't. Her *mamm* had saved his *kinder*, but hadn't been able to reach her daughter. The moment Betty Jane's funeral was over, he'd put Sam and Angela in his buggy, tossed in the few things they had scavenged from the embers and driven away. He hadn't cared where he was going as long as it was away from his mother-in-law, whom he couldn't forgive for forgetting about a pan of oil on the kitchen stove.

For the first year, he'd found work where he could, never staying in one place long. When he'd been hired to help renovate a historical house in Indiana, he'd found a skill he hadn't imagined God would give him. He could paint beautiful patterns he hadn't known were within him. He understood the irony of discovering such an amazing gift after losing his beloved wife.

Mollie expected an answer. Noah glanced at his paint-stained clothes and wished he could postpone this conversation until after he got a *gut* night's sleep, though he couldn't recall the last time he'd had one. They'd had to leave his last job in Wisconsin quickly to catch the train west. He needed a shower, a shave and clean clothes. What must Mollie Lehman think of them?

The door opened, saving him from having to find an answer. An *Englisch* woman walked in. She was slender and dressed in jeans and a short-sleeved shirt. Her long, black hair was piled on top of her head in a messy bun. When she smiled, lines at the corners of her eyes told him it was a common expression for her.

"Are you Noah Frye?" she asked in a serene voice.

"Ja."

Before he could say more, the woman said, "I'm Adelina Marquez, but everyone calls me Lynny."

"Doktor Lynny?" Noah looked toward Mollie.

"Mollie calls me that, but you don't have to." Her smile suggested she was casual about most things in her life other than her work.

Or so he assumed. He couldn't make snap judgments. He needed to be careful whom he trusted. That was a lesson he'd learned in the aftermath of the fire.

"Hi, Mollie," the veterinarian continued. She smiled as Sam crawled into his chair and ran his finger along his plate for the last crumbs. "Hi, everyone! When my guests didn't show up as expected, I called the car service. They connected me with your driver, Noah, and he described where he'd dropped you off, so I knew where you'd be." Her smile widened as she took in the half-eaten pie. "I see Mollie's been taking good care of you."

"Would you like some pie, *Doktor* Lynny? *Mamm*'s coconut-custard." Mollie's smile had returned, but questions filled her eyes when she glanced at him.

"No thanks. I need to get home. Are you ready to go, Noah?"

"Ja." He was more than ready to get out of there. If he stayed, he'd have to answer Mollie's question. *"Danki*, Mollie, for the pie."

"My pleasure," she said, but her voice was as strained as his.

"Let's go, kids," he said.

Angela slid off her chair, but Sam refused to move.

Noah couldn't help being embarrassed when his five-year-old son announced, "You said, when we got out of the car that we were here." He crossed his arms on his narrow chest.

"I *thought* we were where we were supposed to be." Noah hefted his backpack and held out his son's.

Sam didn't take it. He gave his *daed* a defiant scowl.

"*Komm mol*, Sam," Noah said, gesturing toward the back door. "We can talk about this on the way."

"Don't want to go." He reached for his fork. "Want to stay and have pie."

As Noah drew in a deep breath to remonstrate with his son, Mollie asked, "Didn't you know? You can take the rest of pie with you."

"Really?" asked Sam, his eyes wide and his bluster vanishing.

"Really?" echoed his sister, who'd stayed silent during the exchange.

"Of course. *Doktor* Lynny and her husband, Carlos, will be happy to share it with you. Won't that be fun?"

He watched the youngsters lock eyes. They used a silent sibling language he'd never deciphered. As one, they nodded and rushed into the living room to get their roller suitcases.

Doktor Lynny said, "We've got your rooms ready, Noah, and checked off almost everything you requested."

"Almost everything?" he asked. His list of what he needed to take the job hadn't been long. A place to live, transportation to the various sites where the completed barn quilts would be hung and someone to watch over his *kinder* while he worked. At previous jobs, he'd used a small section of his workspace for them. They'd protested in Wisconsin, telling him they were too big to be put in what they described as a playpen. They wanted to be able to run around like other kids. He knew they weren't wrong, which was why he'd added the request to his list.

The veterinarian smiled as she turned to Mollie, who was putting the pie into a box. "Mollie, are you still looking for a job this summer?"

"Ja." She smiled. "Do you know of one?"

Before *Doktor* Lynny could reply, a howl rose from the other room. Sam!

Noah was so tired, he was passed by Mollie and the *Englischer. Doktor* Lynny reached his son first, but astonished him by stepping aside when Mollie kneeled beside him.

Sam was lying on the floor, holding his left leg as if it was broken. His sister had tears in her eyes. Mollie offered her a consoling smile before smoothing Sam's hair from his forehead.

"Did you trip over my brother's shoe?" Mollie asked.

"Ja." The boy managed to answer and groan at the same time.

"Are you hurt?"

"My knee. It went bang."

"Ouch," she murmured.

Sam nodded.

"Big ouch or little ouch?"

"Big..." He paused. "Little ouch."

Mollie smiled. "That's *gut* to hear. That means the ouch will be gone soon, but I'll tell Kolton he needs to pick up his shoes. I'll tell him...again." She smiled, stood and held out her hand to Sam. "If he doesn't listen to me, I'll get you to tell him!"

Sam scrambled to his feet, his bumped knee forgotten. "I'll tell him. I'll tell him real *gut*."

"Me, too?" asked Angela, her eyes wide.

Mollie nodded and gave each *kind* a quick hug. They grinned as if they'd never been embraced before, then threw their arms around her again.

Noah looked away as guilt flooded him.

"She's a schoolteacher," *Doktor* Lynny whispered. "She's amazing with children." Raising her voice, she added, "Noah, like I said, we've taken care of everything on your list except one thing. Childcare. That's why I wanted to talk to you, Mollie. Noah needs a nanny, and you need a job this summer." She smiled at Noah. "Who better to watch your children than a schoolteacher?"

His *kinder* jumped with excitement at the idea, and the veterinarian was grinning. He shifted his gaze to Mollie. Her face was blank. Why? Because she didn't want the job or because she did?

He kept his gaze from settling on her right cheek. The *kinder* liked her, and she understood a *kind*'s wants and needs. So why was he hesitating?

That was another question he knew he'd be foolish to answer, so he said, "If Mollie's interested, let's talk about it tomorrow. I need to get two youngsters to bed."

"Are you interested, Mollie?" *Doktor* Lynny asked.

"I—" She stopped in midsentence, then looked at him and raised her chin. In defiance? Of what? Her own face went blank as she said, "I have to check with my family first."

Noah wasn't sure how to respond, so he nodded, praying he hadn't let the veterinarian with her *gut* intentions goad him into a situation he was going to regret. He'd made a huge mistake when he left his *kinder* in his *mamm*-in-law's care. Would it be a bigger mistake to put his *kinder* into the care of a stranger?

Chapter Two

Mamm looked as exhausted as Noah's kids when she entered the kitchen almost two hours later. After coming to her feet from where she'd been at her quilting frame, Mollie pinned the rest of the pieced top into place so it could be quilted, then shoved Kolton's shoe against the wall so nobody else could trip over it. *Mamm* was later than usual, and Mollie had been waiting to get her *mamm*'s thoughts on *Doktor* Lynny's idea about Mollie babysitting Noah's *kinder*. Mollie had been about to accept the offer for the job, but one glance at Noah's face had halted her. He'd looked like a fox backed into a corner, seeking any way to escape. Pain had flashed through his eyes. Pain and uncertainty. And fear.

She'd almost told him if he didn't want her help to say so, though she was in desperate need of a job. And she liked Noah's kids. It'd been clear, even before Noah mentioned how the family had been living, that they'd been raised differently from other plain *kinder*. The lack of respect in Sam's voice when he refused to get out of his chair was something none of her scholars would have considered doing. Amish kids were raised to believe they were vital and cherished, but also part of a team that worked together, no matter what challenges God put before them.

Mamm walked unsteadily. Viola Lehman wasn't tall—

she was several inches shorter than Mollie. Her gray hair was streaked with white, like a mountain peak when stone was visible through the snow. She didn't raise her eyes while she untied her bonnet and handed it to Mollie.

As Mollie hung it by the door, she asked, "Would you like tea, *Mamm*?"

"That would be *wunderbaar, liebling.*" She gripped the edge of the table as if fearing she'd be swept away by an unseen wave.

"Are you dizzy?"

"I'll be fine once I've had something to drink."

Mollie didn't argue, but her *mamm*'s lightheadedness occurred when she was distressed. After filling a glass with cold water, she handed it to *Mamm*, who took several deep gulps while Mollie put the kettle on for tea.

Sitting where she could see her *mamm*'s face, Mollie asked, *"Was iss letz?"*

"Nothing is wrong." *Mamm* drained the glass.

Mollie rose and refilled it. She put it on the table and sat again. "You look disconcerted."

Mamm patted her hand. "You're a *gut* daughter."

"Then let me help you."

"There's nothing you can do." She took a sip and swallowed. "Not unless you want to buy the High Time for Pie Bakery."

"Dolly and Gil are selling their bakery?"

The shop had debuted last year to a lot of excitement. New businesses didn't come to Lost River often. Everyone had been enthusiastic, though many had questioned how Dolly and Gil Yarwood, the young couple who'd bought the building and renovated it, could make a go of the business when they preferred to spend their time on the ski slopes rather than in the kitchen. They'd hired *Mamm* to make pies and Mollie's older brother Tyler to guide them when they went backcountry skiing.

Mamm sighed. "They're closing the bakery and opening an outdoors-adventure shop. They're hoping to hire Tyler to help them."

Mollie's head reeled. Tyler? Working inside all the time? Her older brother tried to spend every possible minute outdoors on his skis or snowboard. In the summer, he could often be found jogging on the country roads.

If Tyler took a full-time job, how would the farm chores get done? Kolton already worked hard feeding their herd of Black Angus cattle and keeping the fences in repair, along with the other tasks around their hundred acres. She couldn't help because she needed a paying job.

She had one, if she was willing to take it. Delaying could mean it slipping through her fingers.

Mollie stood, her chair scraping the wood floor. "Did you unhitch Chester from the buggy?"

"No, not yet. I thought…that is, I intended…" She wrapped her hands around her glass and stared into it. Her head popped up when Mollie walked past her. "Where are you going? To visit Ruthanne and make plans for her wedding?"

"*Mamm*, we aren't supposed to discuss a wedding before it's published." Mollie smiled to take any sting out of her words. Two months ago, her best friend, Ruthanne Geer, had asked Mollie to oversee preparations for her wedding celebration, as well as the day itself. It was an honor to be asked and a huge responsibility, too. Ruthanne's *mamm* was away in Pennsylvania for the birth of her first *kinskind*, and it might be Mollie's only chance to be part of a wedding. No man had given her a second look since the accident, and how could she walk out with a man when she was certain he'd feel betrayed at learning how impossible it would be for her to carry a *boppli* to term?

"The big day is when?" *Mamm* grinned, and Mollie sent up a silent prayer of gratitude that her teasing had lessened her *mamm*'s worry.

"Sixteen weeks, three days and fourteen hours, give or take."

"Enough time for Ruthanne to change her mind then."

"Mamm!"

Shrugging, *Mamm* said, "The Lord implores us to be honest, and Ruthanne could find a better man than Albert Wynes."

"There's talk of him being put in the lot once he's married."

"There's always talk about who should be considered for the next ordination, but…" She waved a hand as if shooing a fly. "I'm tired and don't know half of what I'm saying."

"Rest and enjoy your tea." Mollie put on her black bonnet. "I'm not going over to Ruthanne's. I've got the possibility of a job for the summer, and I want to make sure I don't lose it."

Mamm's brow wrinkled. "What type of job?"

"Taking care of two *kinder*." She explained about Noah and his job, and his need for someone to watch his daughter and son. "They're staying with Carlos and *Doktor* Lynny, so I'm heading over there. Don't worry about supper. I'll make it when I get back."

"Danki, Mollie."

She hugged her *mamm*. "Isn't it amazing how when one door closes, God opens another?"

"A true blessing." She paused, then said, "I know you were planning to write your letter to *The Budget* today, Mollie. Did you get it done?"

"Not yet." She paused and patted her pocket, where she'd hidden the piece of paper from Noah and his *kinder*. "I'll finish when I get home. There will be plenty of time for us to read it over before I put it in the mail tomorrow."

Mamm gave her a smile. "*Gut*. You know I like to read what you've written first."

"You like finding my mistakes." She laughed to keep any sting out of her words.

"The schoolteacher who makes mistakes—"

"Is human." She bent and kissed the top of her *mamm*'s head. "The water must be near a boil. Enjoy your tea while I'm gone."

"You're a *gut* daughter."

Mollie laughed. "You sound like Kolton and Tyler when they want me to make them something special for supper."

"I was thinking of your six-layer taco salad."

"Sounds *wunderbaar*." She rushed to the door, grateful *Mamm* had suggested a simple dish.

Once the last weeks of school were over, Mollie wouldn't have to spend long hours doing lesson preparations for thirty students. Instead, if Noah gave her the job, she'd spend her days watching the Frye *kinder* and helping Ruth-anne with wedding plans.

Mollie added another prayer as she walked to the black buggy waiting past their vegetable garden. If the job worked out, she might soon be able to pay the bills clipped together with a clothespin in her room. She couldn't wait to toss away the last one.

Noah couldn't believe his eyes as he looked around the log cabin where he and his family would be living for three months while he worked in the San Luis Valley. A huge fireplace claimed the wall in front of where he sat on the dark green leather sofa in the great room that had enough space to seat two districts on a church Sunday. Behind him, a kitchen with the latest gadgets glistened in the setting sun. Huge windows offered views of horses grazing in a nearby field and the sawtooth silhouette of the mountains marking the edges of the vast valley. He guessed the transom windows over the bedroom and bathroom doors could be opened in the winter to let heat swirl through the house. Several pairs of antlers were displayed on one wall, along with a bear pelt, and quilts and crocheted afghans hung over the loft railing. A cowhide was arranged beneath a table next to the kitchen.

It was a smaller version of the magnificent house where their hosts lived. *Doktor* Lynny and her husband, Carlos Marquez, had had supper waiting for them, but despite his assertion to Mollie that the pie wouldn't ruin the kids' appetites, neither Sam nor Angela had been interested in food. Seeing they were so tired they couldn't stop yawning, Carlos had led him and the *kinder* to the smaller house, which his host had called the bunkhouse, and bid them pleasant dreams.

Noah listened for sounds from the other side of the bedroom door beneath the loft. Not that he expected to hear any. Angela and Sam had been asleep almost before their heads hit their pillows. He was tired, too, but he couldn't sleep. Too many thoughts raced through his head as he tried to make sense of what had gone on today.

Why hadn't he immediately agreed to *Doktor* Lynny's suggestion for Mollie to watch his *kinder*? He'd asked himself that over and over on the ride to the horse ranch. He couldn't ignore God's hand in allowing him to meet Mollie and to watch Sam and Angela interact with her. She seemed competent, but was she?

Mollie Lehman was a puzzle he shouldn't be interested in solving. He needed to focus on his *kinder* and his work. Yet there was something intriguing about how she didn't try to hide her scars. Not that plain folk focused on outward appearances. Yet, if he had such scars, he'd be self-conscious.

What had happened to her? He'd almost asked *Doktor* Lynny, but he wouldn't talk about Mollie behind her back. He was certain that if he'd asked Mollie herself, she would have been candid in her answer.

Not like he was.

His hosts were straightforward. He'd liked Carlos from the moment the burly man, who was as round as he was tall, had stepped out to greet them. He wasn't fat. Quite the opposite. He was a consolidation of muscles gained from years of hard labor. He'd been wearing a cotton shirt, well-broken-in denims, fancy boots and a cowboy hat. The kohl-black mustache under his aquiline nose held Noah's attention. The ends were waxed into curves.

"Are you Noah?" he'd boomed in a voice as large as he was. He'd bent toward the youngsters and smiled. "I can see this Noah comes with creatures two by two, too. I can't welcome you to the Ark, but welcome to the Agua Estrella Ranch."

"Water Star Ranch," Noah had said, translating for his *kinder*.

"We know that, *Daed*." Angela had rolled her eyes. "Remember? Mrs. Horner taught us Spanish in Wisconsin." Pulling her hand out of his, she'd taken a step toward the big man. *"¡Hola, señor!"*

"Hola! ¿Hablan español?"

The little girl had switched to English. "Me and Sammy do. *Daed* doesn't."

Sam had asked, "Are we *here* now?"

Jo Ann Brown
31

After Noah had explained how they'd been left at the Lehmans', Carlos had laughed. "Don't feel bad, Noah. Your driver wasn't the first to make that mistake."

"Mollie gave us pie," Sam had interjected.

"I'm not surprised," their host had said. "The Lehmans are hospitable, though they've weathered big storms."

Noah had been curious if Carlos was talking about the actual weather or a different sort of storm. As *Doktor* Lynny had herded them inside to have supper, he'd wondered if his host had been talking about Mollie's injuries. Again, he'd almost asked, but didn't want a reputation as a nosy gossip. He'd been the focus of too much speculation himself.

He tried to persuade his shoulders to relax, but they remained tense. When his stomach grumbled, he knew he should make himself a sandwich from the groceries in the pantry. He didn't get up. He was caught in a strange space between the end of one job and the beginning of the next—it was a place he hated.

God, he prayed, *keep me busy so I don't have to think about anything but patterns for the barn quilts.*

A knock came at the door. An answer from God? He chuckled as he pushed himself to his feet. God didn't work that way. His methods needed to be sought with the heart. That's why Noah had a such a hard time connecting with his Heavenly Father. Since the fire, he'd kept his heart shut. He didn't dare to unlock it. If he did, he'd collapse under the weight of his guilt and anger.

The door opened before Noah could reach it. His eyes widened when Mollie Lehman poked her head around it. "Am I disturbing you?"

He shook his head. "Sam and Angela are asleep in the bedroom."

"Gut." She held out a covered casserole dish. *"Doktor* Lynny asked me to bring this over in case you're hungry." Aromas of chili powder and cumin wafted from it, bringing his taste buds to life. "It's her chili, something that shouldn't be missed."

Had the sound of his stomach's growling reached the big house? He took the dish. *"Danki* for bringing it over."

"I was coming this way, anyhow, so I saved *Doktor* Lynny a few steps. She's busy this time of year with new foals. She must be worn out."

"That condition is infecting everyone."

She laughed, the sound like crystal sunshine. "It'll get worse, I'm afraid, with the lengthening days."

"Do you want to have some chili?" He set the casserole on the table near the kitchen.

"No, *danki*. I need to get home and make supper for *Mamm* and my brothers, but I wanted to tell you I'd be glad to watch Angela and Sam while you paint." She didn't give him a chance to respond before she went on. "I've got lots of experience with *kinder*. I've been teaching school for more than five years. I started after I healed from the accident."

Her words gave him the opportunity he'd been waiting for, but he didn't ask the questions that teased him. If he did, she'd have every right to query about his past. He didn't want to talk about Betty Jane's death and the decisions he'd made before and after the fire.

"If you'd like to talk to the school-board members," she said when he didn't reply, "I can give you their names and addresses." Her easy smile returned.

"That's not necessary. *Doktor* Lynny and Carlos have given you glowing recommendations."

She lowered her eyes, and he wondered if she was pleased

or embarrassed by the praise. When he told her what he'd been authorized to pay for *kinder* care, her head jerked up.

"Is that acceptable?" he asked, having no idea what the usual pay was in Colorado.

"*Ja*. When would you like me to start?"

"Tomorrow, if you can."

Her smile wavered, then her expression steadied. "I've got school this week and next, but there's no reason why the *kinder* shouldn't join us. The scholars are getting ready for their year-end program, and they'll enjoy having an audience. Was Angela preparing anything for the program at the school she went to in…?"

"Wisconsin," he said, then added, "She wasn't attending school there."

"I thought she said she was six."

"She is, but…" It was his turn to drift into silence when he saw her astonishment. "Our host was homeschooling her *kinder*, and she offered to include Angela when she was at the house."

"Where was she the rest of the time?"

"With me."

"In your studio?"

"*Ja*, or where I was hanging the barn quilts."

"She should have been in school each day." Dismay sliced through her voice. "Can she read? Does she know her letters? How to write her name?"

Noah's shoulders ached when he fought to keep them from shrugging. He had no idea how much progress his daughter had made over the past year. She loved looking at books. Was she reading or just enjoying the illustrations?

"I can test her proficiency," Mollie said. "If necessary, I can work with her this summer so she's prepared for second grade in the fall."

"You'd do that?"

"Of course." She regarded him as if he'd grown an extra nose. "No *kind* should have to struggle unnecessarily. If Angela hasn't learned the basics, she'll have to be put into the same grade as her brother. That can create problems."

"Twins—"

"Twins have worked out how to do the same thing on the same schedule by the time they're ready for school. Other siblings haven't. They're accustomed to one being older or younger. Angela *and* Sam will do better if they are kept within their own grades."

"I had no idea."

"Most parents don't." Her warm smile returned. "That's why they depend on schoolteachers for advice." Motioning toward the table, she said, "Enjoy your supper. You can drop off the *kinder* after nine tomorrow. That will give me time to let the scholars know we're having guests." She reached for the knob. "Oh, Carlos has a buckboard you can borrow tomorrow. He can give you directions, too. The school is easy to find. See you then." With a wave, she was gone.

Noah didn't move as the door closed. He heard her footsteps on the porch, then silence. He stayed where he was, feeling as if he'd been flattened by a steamroller. He should be grateful Mollie had anticipated his questions and concerns, but he wondered how long it would take before they butted heads. He had his ways that worked with the *kinder*.

If it's working so well, his conscience asked, *how is it that you don't know if your own daughter can read? Why aren't you grateful for Mollie's offer to help instead of grousing about it?*

He hated questions he didn't know how to answer, and now he had two more.

Chapter Three

Mollie's first opportunity to talk with her older brother, Tyler, was at breakfast the next morning. *Mamm* had left to make her deliveries, and Kolton was heading out to the south pasture to work on the fence. The cattle hadn't escaped yet, but it was only a matter of time before one tried to slip out.

Tyler was finishing his *kaffi* and the final blueberry muffin. She poured herself another cup of tea, because unlike the rest of her family she didn't drink *kaffi*. Sitting at the table, she appraised him.

He was as tall as Noah Frye, but his hair was light brown where Noah's was dark. Tyler's eyes were the pale blue of the heart of a glacier instead of deep brown. Telling herself to stop comparing him to Noah—to stop thinking of Noah at all—she watched Tyler savor each bite of his muffin. His deep tan and rugged muscles caught the attention of her unmarried friends. She'd heard an *Englisch* woman describe him as a fantasy ski bum. When Mollie discovered the term meant a guy who lived to be on the slopes, she knew it was the perfect description for her brother.

Which was why she needed to talk to him before she headed for school and her first day of taking care of the Frye *kinder*.

"I heard the Yarwoods are closing their bakery," she said

as she lifted her cup to her lips. It was too hot to sip, but it allowed her to look over it without staring at him.

"Gil says Dolly was never cut out to be a baker. She doesn't like getting up early, and she's…" He grinned. "How did he put it? Oh, yeah. He says she's as testy as a grumpy old nanny goat before noon. He's going to change the place to something that'll appeal to him and his friends."

"Quite the change from bakery to sports-equipment shop."

"*Ja*, but if it's what they're meant to do, why not?" He swigged the last of his *kaffi* and set down the cup with a thump. "Did *Mamm* tell you that they're interested in me working with them?"

"Will you?" she asked.

"I haven't said no, if that's what you mean."

"You'd be miserable being stuck between four walls, six days a week."

He stuffed the last of the muffin into his mouth, then said, "The money is *gut*, Mollie. Kolton can handle the farm this summer if he doesn't go to Leadville with the youth group at the end of July."

"He's been looking forward to that for months."

"I know, but we're all pitching in to pay the bills this summer. You're going to be watching the painter's kids instead of taking time off to tend your garden as you'd love to do."

She hadn't realized her brother had guessed that. "Tyler, I'm going to be paid well for watching the *kinder*." She shared the number Noah had given her.

"For three months?"

She shook her head. "For every two weeks."

He whistled as he stood. "That's more than generous, Mollie, but it doesn't change anything."

"Of course, it does. If you don't want to take a job at the store, you—"

"*Daed* left me in charge." Tyler reached for his straw hat. "His last words to me were—"

"'Take care of your *mamm*, and follow the path God has given you.' The same thing he told me."

"*Ja.*" He took a deep breath. "I'm thinking about the job, Mollie."

"Will you tell me what you decide before you tell Dolly or Gil?"

"Sure." He gave her a pat on the shoulder. "Don't worry, little sis. If I take the job, I don't intend to keep it too long. I've got other plans."

"Like?"

"Like plans that are my business. Not yours."

She laughed, curious if Tyler had found someone to walk out with. If so, he'd tell her when he was ready. Then Ruthanne's wedding might not be the only one she'd help with…

As her brother went out the door, she glanced at the clock and gasped. If she didn't clear the table and wash the dishes in ten minutes, she'd be late for school. That would be unacceptable any day, but much worse today when the Frye *kinder* were coming. If the exacting Noah decided she was irresponsible, he might fire her. She wouldn't find another job that paid as well. Despite everything she and her *mamm* made and what her brothers earned and the farm's tiny profits, it might not be enough, and they could lose everything.

Every chair scraped on the floor as the door opened at the rear of the schoolroom. Mollie should have known telling her thirty scholars not to stare at the Fryes would be for naught. Noah was an hour late, and the youngsters had been growing anxious for the break in their routine with every passing second. She'd had to chide two of the older scholars to do their desk work. Their squirming and whispering incited the younger *kinder*.

Now, the Fryes had arrived. It was clear Angela and Sam had never seen the inside of a plain school. They looked from the scholars' desks to hers on its raised platform. They stared at the blackboard and the posters on the walls, and the hats and bonnets hung by the door. The cubbyholes where the scholars stored their plastic lunch boxes fascinated the Frye *kinder*.

"*Komm* in," Mollie said as she walked between the rows of desks, trying to ignore how at the moment she'd seen Noah at the door her heart had begun leaping like a mountain goat. "We've been looking forward to your arrival." She gave the slightest motion, and two scholars jumped to their feet and joined her. "This is Enos." She put her hand on the seven-year-old boy's shoulder before doing the same with the eight-year-old girl by her side. "This is Vesta. They'll show you where to store your stuff and where to sit."

Sam and Angela stepped forward when Vesta and Enos held out their hands. Within seconds, the four were chattering like squirrels.

Realizing Noah remained in the doorway, she went to ask if he had any questions. He did. He wanted to know how she was going to test his daughter's reading and math skills.

Mollie kept her gaze on the top button on his shirt so she didn't find herself tumbling into his dark eyes while she reassured him the *kinder*'s day would be focused on getting to know the other kids. Going with him outside, where they could talk without being overheard, she said, "I want to gauge how Angela interacts with others her age."

"That makes sense."

"I try to be sensible." *Gut!* Keep everything light and

cheerful. That way, he wouldn't guess her dreams last night had been filled with imaginary conversations as she and Noah had strolled together.

He started to retort, then must have seen her smile because he let whatever he'd been about to say slide out in a gentle sigh. "Sorry, Mollie. I shouldn't be questioning you."

"Why not? You're their *daed*. You've got every right to know what they're learning and how. I encourage parents to ask questions. Doing that avoids misunderstandings when what the scholars repeat to their parents isn't close to what I meant for them to share."

A faint smile tipped his lips. "I get the message. Don't assume."

She glanced over her shoulder at a burst of laughter from inside. "I need to go."

"I understand. I've got meetings today, and I'm late for the first one." He grimaced. "The day didn't start off well because Sam didn't want to leave the house."

"He was scared of coming to school?"

"I think he's too tired." He covered a yawn, then waved it aside as if he could make it disappear. "It's going to take time to catch up on sleep."

Sympathy cut through the guardrails she'd put in place around her heart, and she knew she had to keep everything between them professional. "Noah, I need you to be on time from this point forward, both in the morning and the afternoon. I don't want *Mamm* to have to begin supper on her own."

"I understand."

She realized he did. *"Danki."*

"I'll make sure I'm here on time. If—"

Another swell of laughter, louder this time, made her cut him off with a wave before she hurried inside and shut the door. She walked to the front of the room, calling the fifth graders forward to be drilled on their spelling words. She knew, as her ears strained for the sound of the wagon heading to the road, that concentrating on the scholars was going to be more difficult than she'd expected when she'd invited Noah to drop off his *kinder*.

Much more difficult.

As Noah returned to the schoolhouse that afternoon, he was aware he'd broken his word to Mollie twice today. He seldom wished he had a motorized vehicle, but today he did. A car would have made short work of the ten miles from his meeting with the arts council in Lost River. He'd been offered a ride to pick up the kids, but knew someone would have to return for the horse and wagon. He'd thanked them before leaving… Or when he thought he'd be leaving. Two of the commissioners had cornered him outside the meeting space. Brant Hunter was the council's chairman, and Wendy Warner served as his vice chair. They'd peppered him with questions—most of which had already been discussed. He wasn't sure if they hadn't liked his answers or if they were confirming he meant what he'd said.

He was almost an hour late returning to the schoolhouse. He breathed a prayer of gratitude when he saw the small building in the distance. The light tan structure with a porch across the front and a bell hanging to one side of the door could have been the school he'd attended in Lancaster County. Only this one was set amid sagebrush and cottonwoods. The double outhouses, the cylindrical propane tank and the scuffed ball field were identical. He couldn't remember seeing a lean-to stable in Pennsylvania. The greater distances here must mean *kinder* used horses.

As he turned his borrowed wagon toward the school,

he chided himself for getting so caught up in the meeting with the arts council that he'd failed to keep an eye on the time. Their plans and the part Noah would play in them had been fascinating, but Noah had told Mollie he wouldn't be late, yet he was.

Again.

He saw three forms on the porch. Mollie was sitting with his *kinder*.

She wouldn't abandon them. That voice reminding him not to be negative rang through his head. *You've seen how much she cares about others.*

For the second time in two days, he was intruding on her time. She must have tasks at day's end for the school, as well as work when she got home. He heard the sweet sound of his daughter's laugh, followed by his son's. Sam and Angela were enjoying whatever they were talking about.

"I'm so sorry I'm late." Noah stepped out of the wagon.

Mollie smoothed her apron as she stood. "We've been getting to know each other better."

He wanted to ask what his *kinder* had spilled about their fractured family, but didn't, as Sam and Angela told Mollie goodbye.

"Not so fast," Noah said as he followed in their wake. "We've made Teacher Mollie late. The least we can do is help her clean up."

"That's not necessary," she said, but he saw gratitude in her eyes.

For the first time, he wondered if her scars were painful. He bit back the question, figuring she'd despise it as much as he did the sympathy everyone had wanted to heap on him after Betty Jane's death.

"I think it is," he replied.

"I've got a couple of tasks you can do." She put up a

hand to halt him from answering. "You've had a long day, I can tell, Noah, and it's not over."

"Is it that obvious?" he asked as he followed her into the school. The interior resembled the school he'd attended so much that nostalgia threatened to sweep him into the past, long before grief had taken over his life.

She didn't answer while she led the *kinder* down the single aisle between the desks. He counted thirty desks, and each one had been in use. So many scholars would require her attention every second of the day.

Sam paused in front of a childish picture on the wall and announced it'd been drawn by Enos. Noah nodded as his son outlined everything *wunderbaar* about his new friend. Enos had traded half his strawberry-jam sandwich for half of the tuna sandwich Noah had packed for Sam. Not only that, but Enos had also gotten his spelling words correct the first time.

"Except three," Sam said.

"How many did he have?" Noah asked, delighted his son was so animated.

"Five."

Struggling not to let his reaction show, Noah's gaze cut to Mollie, who was trying not to smile, either.

"Mollie helped him," Sam went on, "and he got every one right the second time."

"That's *gut*, ain't so?" Noah asked.

"Angela got all her spelling words right the first time." Sam's chest thrust out as if he'd been the one who'd mastered a list of words.

"Five words?" Noah asked.

"Ten!" Sam spun to his sister. "Isn't that right, Angela?"

Mollie asked Angela and Sam to clean the erasers. "Stand with your backs to the wind," she cautioned as they grabbed them off the tray by the blackboard and ran toward the door. "Otherwise, you'll be spitting out chalk dust until breakfast tomorrow."

As the door slammed closed behind them, Noah said, "That sounds like the voice of experience."

"It is." She smiled. "They both did well today."

"I didn't think you were going to test Angela."

"I didn't, but she wanted to participate, so I gave her first-grade spelling words. As Sam said, she got them correct."

"That's *gut*, ain't so?"

Mollie nodded. "It's very *gut*." She glanced toward the door as it reopened. "Put the erasers by the chalk and then you can help me and your *daed* check that the windows are closed and locked."

As Sam trotted after her like a well-trained pup, Noah motioned for his daughter to come with him to the other side of the room. Sam prattled about everything he'd experienced that day. Mollie smiled as she tested the five windows on the far side. Each motion the blonde schoolteacher made resonated through Noah as if she'd brushed him with the bristles of the broom she got from a closet.

It was less than five minutes later when, after gathering the dust and carrying it to the door, she said, "*Danki*. Many hands make quick work, ain't so?"

Noah was about to reply when he realized she was talking to Angela and Sam. Each of his senses had been focused on Mollie instead of on his kids. That couldn't happen again.

How are you going to stop it?

Wanting to tell that rational voice to be quiet, he was about to ask his *kinder* to get their things and join him in the wagon. He didn't get a chance.

"One last thing," Mollie said. "Angela and Sam, will you

go and make sure all of the softball equipment has been brought inside?"

They almost ran over him in their haste to do as Mollie asked.

"How do you do it?" He walked toward where she was setting her bonnet over her *kapp*. "I never get them to help with such enthusiasm."

"You don't have extra spelling words you can give them," she said as she tied it under her chin.

"You threaten the scholars with extra spelling words?" he asked, shocked.

"*Ja*, but they love it. If they can learn extra spelling words, they get a star in my book. The more stars they get each week, the bigger the piece of cake *Mamm* makes for them each Friday. The most reluctant scholar will put in extra effort for my *mamm*'s cake."

"After tasting her pie, I have to assume her cake must be amazing."

"More than you can imagine." She gestured toward the door. "*Danki* for your help."

"I apologize again for being delayed."

Again she perceived what he didn't say. "How's the quilt trail project doing?"

"I'm meeting a lot of people who have a lot of ideas." Hearing his *kinder* squeal from the side of schoolyard, he glanced over to see them chasing each other around the bases.

Mollie sat on the edge of the porch again, and he did the same. He appreciated her allowing Sam and Angela to play. Wearing themselves out would make it easier to get them to bed tonight.

"Isn't it *gut* so many people are interested in the project?" she asked, watching the *kinder*, too. She seemed more content at school than she'd been at either her house or the ranch.

"*Ja.* Having community support is great. What isn't great is that everyone has an opinion of what the project should be, and so far, no two opinions are the same."

"Including yours?"

He drew in a deep breath and let it ease out. "I've been working on barn quilts for three years, but they act as if I've never picked up a paintbrush."

Her laugh lilted through the afternoon air. "You're in Colorado, Noah. We work well together when we find common ground, but it takes a lot of compromise to get to that common ground."

"I'm seeing that. Everywhere else I've worked, the barn quilts have been influenced by traditional quilt squares. Here? Some want traditional quilt squares, but others want barn-quilt squares that reflect, and I quote, 'the diverse history of the San Luis Valley.'"

"I think the latter group is right."

He pulled his gaze from his kids. "You do?"

"*Ja.* This valley has been settled over and over through time. The Indigenous people, the Spanish conquistadors, the gold rushers on their way to California, the Mexicans who came north through New Mexico and the other Americans and immigrants who were seeking a place to settle where they weren't living cheek-by-jowl with their neighbors. The Amish have come here along with those who want to live off the grid and the city people who want to live near the mountains so they can ski in the winter and fish in the summer."

"I ask a simple question, and you give me an answer worthy of an encyclopedia."

"It's because I'm a teacher."

"Or is it an excuse for you to share what you're excited about?"

She chuckled again. "You're right. I love Lost River and the whole valley. I look for ways to make others love it, too." Before he could warn her that her efforts would be wasted on him, because this was temporary for him and his *kinder*, she added, "The idea of the barn quilts reflecting the peoples of the valley is a *wunderbaar* one."

"Except I don't know where to start to look for patterns."

"That's easy. Ask me. I belong to a quilt circle, and we've made quilts based on southwestern and Indigenous textile patterns."

He stared at her in amazement. If he'd had any doubts before, he could see why God had brought him to her doorstep. "I'd like that," he said, overwhelmed with her generosity. *God,* danki *for putting this unexpected assistance right in my path.*

"Gut." She rose as Angela and Sam ran to them. Gathering the equipment they'd collected, she said, "I'll see you tomorrow."

"We can visit again?" asked Sam, who was so excited he bounced from one foot to the other.

"Ja. Every day this week."

His son cheered.

Mollie bid them a pleasant evening. He told her to have the same before herding his kids toward the wagon. Glancing over his shoulder, he could almost see the roots that connected Mollie to this valley and the people within it.

"Daed," Angela said, "I like Mollie."

"I do, too," he said, then clamped his lips closed before he could say something else stupid.

As if she was the parent, Angela patted his arm before climbing into the wagon. He had to force his feet to follow instead of turning around so he could ask Mollie to join him and the *kinder* for supper.

To talk about quilt patterns. Nothing more, he tried to convince himself, but he couldn't.

After swinging into the wagon and making sure both kids were seated safely, he grasped the reins. He drove along the lane to the county road. He refused to let himself look back or to ask himself why he'd had a sudden pulse of envy when he thought of how Mollie looked comfortable at her school. She represented everything he'd lost: parents and siblings and familiar faces he'd known his whole life, as well as a sense of being where he should be.

The place where he belonged.

He hadn't felt at home anywhere since the fire and wondered if he ever would again.

Chapter Four

The following week, Mollie watched with pleasure as Sam and Angela became accustomed to being with the other scholars. They didn't have any more interest than the rest of the *kinder* in studying when the bright sunshine and warm weather teased them to play. Their gazes slipped time after time toward the windows on either side of the classroom. She sent the youngsters out for a fifteen-minute break halfway through the morning, giving them time to play on the swings.

Mollie looked up, surprised, when the front door opened. She glanced out the right-hand windows. The scholars were enjoying their free time and were within sight. That was one of the first rules she taught them. They couldn't go wandering off across the field, with its scraggly plants, where a rattlesnake might have a nest. Most *kinder* understood that by the time they got to school, but a few needed to be reminded.

"I hope I'm not interrupting," called a familiar voice.

Mollie stood behind her desk. "Ruthanne! I didn't expect to see you today."

Her friend was a slip of a woman, fine-boned and hardly taller than the oldest scholars at Mollie's school. Her cheekbones were high and sharp, and complemented her dark brown eyes and black hair. Anyone who thought to dismiss Ruthanne because she was small soon learned she had strong opinions and never hesitated to express them. Mollie admired that about her friend.

"I told you I'd help with the program practice, ain't so?" Ruthanne took off her black bonnet and put it on a peg by the door. She adjusted her white cone-shaped *kapp* and smiled.

"Ja." She hid her astonishment from her friend. Practice for the presentations had been going on for two weeks, and Ruthanne hadn't stepped foot in the school.

Mollie chided herself. Her friend was busy. Ruthanne's *mamm* was in Lancaster County, taking care of her older daughter as well as her first *kins-kind*. In her absence, Ruthanne had the full responsibility for her family's home, cleaning, doing laundry and cooking meals for her *daed*, six brothers and *grossdawdi*. She didn't have a moment to call her own.

A couple of times each week, Ruthanne came to the Lehmans' house and went over questions and wedding plans with Mollie. They'd laugh and quilt while they talked about what flavor cakes Ruthanne wanted for her wedding dinner, as well as the important issue of which unmarried girl would sit with which unmarried man at the wedding supper. Ruthanne was determined to get Mollie the best partner for the meal, but Mollie changed the subject each time her name came up. Nothing could alter the truth that Mollie was destined to become an *alt maedel*. The boys who used to flirt with her had married other women—women without a trio of scars marring their faces.

Mollie went out to the porch to ring the school bell. Most of the scholars had started for the school before the first peal rang across the sunny fields. Their eager voices drowned out the baaing of the sheep next door at the Detweiler farm. By the time the first scholars crowded past her and into the school, the rest had joined them.

She smiled at each one. When a small hand slipped into hers, she looked at Sam, who grinned at her with a dirty face. The little boy attracted dirt like chalk dust to a black apron. He held her hand until they were inside, then he scurried to the desk he shared with Enos. The two bowed their heads toward each other, whispered, then giggled when Mollie announced it was time to practice the presentation again. She'd suspected the scholars would be bored with it, but realized they preferred that to arithmetic or spelling.

With Ruthanne's help, everything went smoothly. Each *kind* remembered his or her place in the three rows. No one forgot their turn to recite or sing. The hymns beginning and ending the exercises were on pitch and on time, and nobody disrupted the music with whispers.

Mollie prayed everything would be as *gut* in three days, when the presentation would be followed by a family picnic in the yard. She thanked the scholars for their hard work before sending them home. As she did each day, she watched while the youngsters got their horses or ponies or bikes. Soon, the gravel drive was busy with kids heading in every direction.

When she turned toward her desk, only the Frye *kinder* and Ruthanne remained. She gave Angela and Sam the task of clapping the erasers. As soon as they'd gone outside, she thanked her friend while closing the books on her desk and putting them in drawers.

Ruthanne went to the nearby closet and pulled out the broom and dustpan. Sweeping around the desks, she said, "I know I told you I'd be here more often, but—"

"You don't need to explain. I know how tough it can be to pick up after two brothers and keep house. You've got six."

"Plus *Daed* and *Grossdawdi*." She stopped and leaned on the broom. "I'm not complaining. Well, not too much."

A grin stole across her face before she grew serious again. "I'm sorry, Mollie. I should have been here before."

"You're here today, and I'm grateful for that. I'd love to have you over for supper soon. *Mamm* and Tyler and Kolton enjoy seeing you. You could bring Albert, too." She paused. "I can't remember the last time I spent time with both of you."

Straightening, Ruthanne frowned. "I mentioned to him the last time we went for a walk that he has to get past what's bothering him about you."

"About me?"

"*Ja*, if I mention your name, he changes the subject so fast my head spins. As far as joining you for supper, let me see if I can make that work."

Mollie let Ruthanne go on. She and Albert Wynes had been friends and neighbors before Mollie first met Ruthanne. Once, she and Albert been inseparable as they shared a horse to and from school. She'd played ball with Albert, his brothers and her own. With his sisters, she'd caught kittens in the barn and colored and cut out paper dolls. The family had moved to a bigger farm north of Lost River, but she'd seen him at youth events. There had been attempts before her accident to make a match for her and Albert, but they'd viewed each other as friends, nothing more.

Now he acted as if she'd vanished from his life. He spoke to her during church services when required. Though Ruthanne hadn't said much, Mollie had the impression Albert wasn't happy Ruthanne had chosen her as one of the two *newehockers* who would stand beside her while Ruthanne spoke her wedding vows.

Why? Had something occurred to sour him toward her before or during the aftermath of Mollie's accident? That time was lost to her, as if it'd never happened.

Mollie puzzled over that while she finished cleaning after Ruthanne left for home. Angela and Sam did their best to help, and she was grateful they were willing to sharpen pencils and return the small library's books to their shelves. In fact, with their help, it took her only fifteen minutes longer to do her chores than if she'd been there by herself.

No matter. She had plenty of time to get them home before Noah returned. He'd had meetings every day since he'd arrived, and though he hadn't said anything, his *kinder* had, so she knew he was frustrated with the ongoing discussions when he wanted to get to work.

When she arrived at the ranch with the youngsters, Mollie looked for Carlos and *Doktor* Lynny, but neither was around.

"Komm mol," cried Sam as he jumped out of the buggy the moment it stopped. "You need to see our new house."

House. Not home. How many times had Noah moved the *kinder* from one place to another? She scolded herself. Why would she expect his kids to think of the ranch as home so soon? She was looking for problems where there might not be any.

She went into the house with Angela and Sam. The *kinder* gave her enough time to put down her purse before they announced they were starving. Finding a cake mix in the pantry, she mixed the chocolate batter, filled the pans and put them in the oven.

"Those should be ready in a half hour," she said. "Will you show me around your new bedroom while we wait?"

The kids grabbed her hands and tugged her into the room beneath the loft.

"Here's our room," Sam announced as he flung out his arms.

Mollie should have been used to a messy room. Neither of her brothers shared her need for order. They believed tossing clothes—dirty and clean mixed together—on a chair or the foot of the bed was the best way to keep their rooms neat, but even that chaos didn't compare to what was in front of her. How could two small *kinder* make such a big mess in just over a week?

Two suitcases and backpacks were shoved into corners. Everything that had been in them was dumped on the beds. Not at the foot, as her brothers did, but across them. Toys were scattered like a maze with no rhyme or reason. Dresser drawers were closed, but the open closet door revealed it was empty.

"How do you get through this room with everything tossed everywhere?" Mollie asked.

Angela looked puzzled. "We need to be able to get to our stuff."

"Wouldn't it be better if it were in its proper place?"

The kids exchanged a baffled glance.

"Put away," Mollie amended. "So you don't walk on it or sleep with it."

"We don't stay anywhere long enough to put things away," Sam said with the self-assurance of a five-year-old. "*Daed* doesn't mind."

Angela wagged a finger at her brother. "*Daed* keeps saying we need to pick up."

"He closes the door and sighs." Sam shrugged. "So I guess he's okay."

"Maybe he is," Mollie said, sure their *daed* had been too tired at day's end to oversee the youngsters cleaning up their room. "I'm not."

Sam frowned and crossed his arms over his narrow chest. "Are you going to make us pick everything up?"

"Not everything. Just the stuff on the floor and on your beds."

"That's *everything*!"

"No," she said, keeping her voice light. "Your shoes can stay where they are, and some toys are in the chest under the window. Shall we get started on the rest?"

Again, the *kinder* exchanged a glance. This one she could read easily. They weren't buying her cheerful tone.

Acting as if she hadn't noticed their silent communication, she scooped up a pile of clothes from the bottom of one bed. She put them on a table and began sorting them. After rolling two matching socks together, she tossed them in a lazy arc into the top open drawer of the dresser.

"Two points." She laughed.

"What?" asked Angela, who was carrying an armful of blocks to the toy chest.

"You get two points for a basket." She spread out the clothing, looking for another pair of socks.

"It's not a basket. It's a drawer." Sam gasped as Mollie sent another set of rolled socks into the drawer.

"It's like basketball, ain't so?"

Both *kinder* regarded her with obvious bafflement.

"Haven't you ever played basketball?" she asked.

They shook their heads.

"Well, it's time you learned. We'll start here." It didn't take her long to describe the game of putting a ball through a net. Once they realized what she meant, the *kinder* were eager to prove they were the better one at a sport they hadn't heard of five minutes ago. Mollie had to halt Sam from throwing toys at the chest except for a soft ball that bounced off the wall and back to him.

"A rebound," she said when he scowled. "That's part of the game. Catching a rebound is something to cheer about."

He smiled while his sister was making short shrift of the socks piled on the beds. Mollie ducked as rolled socks arced into the top drawer and laughed when one struck the ceiling and dropped onto Angela's head. They all laughed as they worked together, pausing only long enough to take the cake layers out of the oven and leaving them to cool. They returned to the bedroom to finish the cleanup, but the kids whirled as the front door opened.

Noah stood in the doorway and stared. Lack of sleep shadowed his eyes, and his lips were drawn into a grim expression.

Before she could greet him, Angela called out, "*Daed!* Look what we've done. Doesn't it look *gut*?"

"I've got more baskets than Angela," Sam crowed.

Mollie was shocked when Noah ignored his *kinder* as he stamped toward her. When he was less than an arm's length from her, she steeled herself not to back away like a frightened rabbit. It wasn't easy when she had no idea why he was upset.

"Why are you in here?"

She couldn't figure out what was behind his question. "I'm here to help the *kinder* clean up their room. Where else would we be?"

He glanced around, his eyes wide, before they narrowed again as he said, "With me in my studio."

"I didn't realize you were there."

"You should have checked when you got here."

"Why?"

"I thought I told you that I wanted them with me in the studio." His sharp voice clipped off each word. "Unless they were at school."

"If you did, your request didn't register with me." She put her hands on either side of her head, contorting her white *kapp*. Keeping her voice light wasn't easy, but she wasn't going to let him suck her into his negativity. "During the last couple of weeks of school, my brain fills up with details of the end-of-the-year program as well as assisting the eighth graders on their way out of school and toward adulthood. I think about which students will need to repeat which subjects next year because they didn't grasp them this year, and how to ease the newest scholars into school in the fall. Everything else bounces off my skull and doesn't stick in my brain."

He hesitated, and she guessed her silliness had reached through his anger to his *gut* sense. When he spoke, his tone wasn't as belligerent. "Is it a problem to watch them in my studio or where I need to go when we're hanging barn quilts?"

Astonished, she realized he was holding his breath as he waited for her answer. Did he fear she'd say no? If she did, was he worried he wouldn't be able to find someone to watch his daughter and son? What he didn't know was how much she needed the generous wages he'd offered.

She was about to blurt out she was willing to watch the *kinder* wherever he wished, but halted herself. Raising her eyes to meet his, she said, "I must be home each day to make supper for my family. Having to do that after baking and making her deliveries is too much for *Mamm*."

"I wish I could assure you every day will go as it should, and you'll be home on schedule." He stuck his hands into his pockets. "What I can tell you is if there's going to be a delay, I'll make sure you get home in time to do your cooking."

"Some days, I may have to take Angela and Sam home with me. You can pick them up when you're done."

Mollie almost gasped when he hesitated. He trusted her with his *kinder* during the school day. What was different about them joining her at her house or his otherwise?

* * *

Knowing he'd come close to revealing the truth he needed to keep hidden, Noah had to find something to cover his faltering...and the pain that lurked in his heart. What would Mollie think of him if she learned he hadn't been there to protect his wife and family?

He didn't want to find out, so he gave an exaggerated yawn. "Sorry, Mollie. All the talk today has bored me to the point I need a nap."

Her smile returned, and it was warm. "I understand. That's why I volunteered to have this summer's teachers' meeting at my house next month. That way, I may have sway in moving the discussion along."

"Let me know if that works." He was able to grin, surprising himself. Anything but a frown had come hard for him since he'd left Pennsylvania. "I might borrow your techniques for these endless meetings. They want to debate and talk and debate more instead of letting me do actual painting."

Angela grabbed his hand. "Let's show Mollie your studio!"

"Would you like to see it?" he asked, astonished how much he hoped she'd agree.

"I should, as I'm going to be spending time with you there."

Noah was shocked anew how delighted he was by her words—words that shouldn't have garnered any response other than relief he'd solved the issue of having someone watch his *kinder* while he worked. Not wanting to let his thoughts dwell on his peculiar reaction, he led the way to his newest studio, which was set to the left of the bunkhouse.

A new studio was one of the hassles of moving from state to state with his work. No two areas he'd been given were identical. He had to figure out where the light was best and how to store his supplies so they were at hand, but not in the way when he was working.

"Wow!" Mollie said from behind him as he opened the carved wooden door. "This doesn't look anything at all like what I expected."

"What did you expect?" He looked around what had once been a small stable and tack area. He was grateful for the pegs along the wall where bridles and halters had hung. It was the perfect place to store his paint. His brushes waited for him in the buckets that used to hold water or grain.

"I don't know, but it looks more like a woodworker's shop."

His table saw waited next to a planer and a belt sander, as well as two different-size hand sanders. "The planer was here when I moved my stuff in. I use the saw to make sections of the barn quilts the proper size. The sanders will keep the edges smooth."

"This is the cleanest stable I've ever seen."

"I know. I wonder how many people worked to scour the floorboards. Marks from horseshoes are in the wood, so there were once horses stabled in here."

Mollie laughed. "You'll learn Carlos and *Doktor* Lynny will never turn away a horse that needs a home. If they don't have room, they build another barn. At last count, they had a dozen."

"Horses?"

"Barns!" She wandered to where the panels he'd use for making the barn quilts were stacked. "This isn't plywood."

"Plywood is too rough, and there are knots that would show through the painting. When the quilt is up on a barn, any distortion becomes obvious. These panels have resin on one side to create a smooth surface." He ran his hand across it and motioned for her to do the same. "It's okay. You won't get a splinter."

She copied his motion. "The board is as silky as a sheet of paper. Where do you get them?"

"From a store where they make and sell signs. That's what this wood is designed for. When Carlos contacted me about a barn-quilt trail in the San Luis Valley, I sent him a list of supplies I'd need." He spread out his arms. "You can see the result."

As his *kinder* went to a small table set aside for their use in one corner, Mollie walked to the closest stall, where he'd stored more boards for the barn quilts. "How many barn quilts will you make out of each of these?"

"I'll need four for each quilt. The standard size of a finished one is eight feet by eight feet."

"That's huge." She leaned on the wall and peered in the stall at the supplies he'd stored there.

"They've got to be seen from the road. That's the whole idea of a barn-quilt trail. The community together builds something that will bring tourists to view the quilts and stop and spend money at the businesses along the way."

Turning to face him, she asked, "How do you decide which pattern to use?"

"Some owners of the barns and buildings where the quilts will be hung have definite ideas of what they want. Others are looking to me for ideas." He gave her a faint smile. "I'm hoping you can help with those."

"Don't worry. My quilting circle has more ideas than we can sew in a lifetime. We'll be glad to make suggestions." She laughed again. "Probably more than you'll want or need. I know you want to get to work, but I need to talk to you about something important."

"I need to talk to you, too."

"*Gut.* I'll start. Angela and Sam want to learn to play basketball. With a real ball instead of socks."

Noah sputtered. Of the million things Mollie could have said, he hadn't imagined she'd consider his *kinder* learning to play a game important. Didn't they know about basketball? It was such a popular sport in Indiana, where they'd lived before his work had taken them to Wisconsin. He'd assumed they knew all about it. Again, Mollie was making him see how little he truly knew about his own *kinder*.

"Are you going to teach them?" he asked. He berated himself for such a stupid question, but how was he supposed to respond when Mollie considered learning a *game* so significant for Angela and Sam?

Yet, he was happy to talk about anything other than her expression when he'd faltered over answering her when she'd offered to take the kids home with her if he had to work late. She was curious why, and he didn't blame her. He should have been delighted with her generosity, but her offer, which would take his kids out of his sight and into her kitchen, frightened him to his marrow.

He'd made a terrible mistake five years ago. He wasn't going to make the same mistake again. This time, the results could be worse.

Chapter Five

❧

"*Daed?*"

Angela's voice barely penetrated through Noah's thoughts as he regarded the empty board in front of him. He'd attended another lengthy meeting today while the *kinder* were in school, and he'd been as antsy as a toddler through the long three hours of listening to debate about what he considered irrelevant details before there were actual completed barn quilts to hang.

He knew he hadn't been as bothered by the topics of discussion as he was with his own thoughts. Though he knew Angela and Sam should be safe at the school, his conversation with Mollie yesterday had lingered and plagued him, making it difficult to take in everything that was said around the table, where the arts commission and others interested in the barn-quilt trail had gathered to decide which buildings should display the first quilts.

They'd looked to him for ideas for quilts. Each one he'd offered was subject to discussion, and several were altered. None had been turned down, which he considered *gut* news. The meeting had come to a close when he offered the suggestion that the first quilt should be hung where the commission wanted the trail to begin. Everyone was in agreement that the trail's first stop should be Lost River's visitors center.

By the time he'd returned to the Marquezes' ranch, his brain was weary. He appreciated Mollie watching Angela and Sam while he got materials together to begin working. He put a piece of plywood on top of two sawhorses to create a large worktable to hold boards for the barn quilts. Once he had the plywood secure, he gathered the small cans of paint he'd need for the first section. In the morning when the light streamed through the windows, he'd begin. Lost in his thoughts, he flinched when Mollie spoke his name, and he realized he'd never answered his daughter.

"What's wrong?" Mollie asked.

"What makes you think something is wrong?"

"You're staring off into space with a scowl."

"Thinking about my projects and how I'll work in this studio."

She scanned the area. "Is there something wrong with it?"

"I don't know. Yet." When she gave him a look that questioned if he'd misplaced his mind, he quickly said, "I've got to see how the light fills this space during the day. In a few days, I should have a better idea."

Mollie nodded, but appeared uncertain. He would happily have spent the next hour explaining how different slants of the sun could change the appearance of colors. He refrained because when he'd spoken to others about it, they'd become bored. Would Mollie? He'd watched her listening to convoluted stories told by his *kinder*. She never appeared to lose interest. Was she feigning attention while her mind was busy with other thoughts?

He'd missed his chance to find out because she went to where Angela and Sam were playing with plastic construction blocks in a corner. Sunshine flowed over the pieces, turning them almost fluorescent. With a sigh, he turned to his worktable. He tried to ignore their laughter and conversation, which teased him to join them.

Again, his opportunity passed him by, because at four, Mollie told them she needed to get home to start supper. He resisted the yearning to ask her into the house. Mollie had made it clear she had a lot to do at home, so she waved to him and the *kinder* as they emerged from the studio barn. Without another word, she drove away.

"Why didn't you ask her to have a glass of lemonade with us, *Daed*?" asked Angela with a glance at her brother, who nodded.

Noah was baffled. "Why would I ask her to have lemonade when we don't have any? That would be rude."

"You could have made some."

"Like the last batch I attempted to make?"

Sam's face screwed up. "You forgot the sugar!"

Noah ruffled his hair. "I won't do that again."

"You should have asked Mollie inside," Angela persisted, "so she can have something to drink before she heads home. It's dusty out here."

"You're right." He was surprised by his young daughter's insight. He shouldn't have been. Betty Jane always had been concerned about others' feelings and needs, one of the many reasons he'd fallen in love with her. Angela must have inherited that from her *mamm*. "We'll ask her in tomorrow. If she has the time."

That satisfied the *kinder*. He led them into the bunkhouse and the kids vanished into their bedroom. He went to the kitchen to check out what he could make for supper, telling himself, as he had for the past two days, that he should go into town and buy groceries. He needed a few more hours in each day and a lot fewer meetings.

He was astonished, after opening the refrigerator door, to

see a casserole with a note written on lined paper perched on top.

"'Warm the taco-salad ingredients in the oven for half an hour at three hundred fifty degrees,'" he said aloud. "'Once it's warm, serve it in the taco shells I put in the pantry. Toppings are in containers behind this pan. Chopped vegetables are in the crisper.'"

It was signed with Mollie's name, which she'd written with broad printed letters. He wondered if she'd developed such a simple signature because she used it with the youngest scholars.

The more important question was…when had she brought the casserole and the other fixings into the house? It must have been in the moments of chaos when his son and daughter had rushed into the studio to tell him about their day at school. With everything she had to do… He was touched by her kindness, in spite of his determination to keep his emotions under tight control.

Forty-five minutes later, he and his *kinder* sat at the table and shared silent grace. His kids were enticed by the delicious, spicy scents and couldn't sit still until he cleared his throat to signal grace was finished. Sam bounced off his chair while he waited for Noah to spoon the mix of spiced hamburger, beans, olives and onions into a crisp taco shell, topping it with generous heaps of guacamole, salsa and sour cream. The little boy giggled as he added his own shredded lettuce, cheese and broken tortilla chips.

Licking his fingers, Sam said, "Save another shell for me. I'm going to want seconds."

"Why don't you finish that one first?" Noah asked as he finished filling a shell for Angela, who wasn't as messy adding toppings to her salad.

Sam couldn't answer because his mouth was full. Both kids were silent as they dug in.

Noah understood why as soon as he took his first bite. The concoction of flavors burst like fireworks on his tongue.

Did Mollie Lehman do everything well? She was a dedicated teacher and helped her *mamm* with their household. And she had such patience with his kids, deflecting anything that might lead to a spat as well as convincing them to pick up their messes. On top of that, she was a superb cook.

"I wish we had this every night," Angela said with a happy sigh as she chased a few beans around the soggy bottom of the taco shell.

"Me, too!" Noah replied before he realized he'd said those words at the same time as Sam had. He patted his son's arm. "I'll get the recipe from Mollie."

The *kinder* exchanged a glance before Angela said, "You don't cook this *gut*, *Daed*."

"If I have her recipe, I might be able to make this."

Sam regarded him as if they'd switched roles as *daed* and son. "Don't forget about the lemonade. You had a recipe for that, ain't so?"

As they laughed, Noah enjoyed his taco salad, then had a second one. Sam decided not to have another. Instead, he helped himself to Noah's. They were all full by the time they thanked God for their delicious supper.

Again, Noah was grateful to Mollie because he didn't have a lot of dishes to wash while the *kinder* put the leftovers away. Mostly Angela, because Sam couldn't reach very high, but he transported the containers from the table under Noah's watchful eye. The little boy could trip over a mote of dust, and Noah didn't want to have to clean guacamole from between the wood floorboards.

As he wiped the last dish dry and placed it in the cupboard, Noah turned to see his daughter sitting in a rocker in the living room. She was holding a newspaper as if she could read every word. Could she? He had no idea how much Angela had learned.

His curiosity led him to check out the name of the newspaper. "Is that *The Budget*? Where did you find a copy of it?"

"Carlos said I could look at it." Her ruddy brow lowered as she stared at the pages.

"Carlos reads *The Budget*?" He didn't expect his daughter to answer the question. He knew non-plain people read the weekly newspaper, but he hadn't imagined a Colorado rancher would.

Angela nodded. "He says it's nice to read *gut* news instead." Her forehead wrinkled. "Instead of what, *Daed*?"

"Instead of sad stories about accidents and forest fires." He hoped that would halt her questions.

It did, because she jabbed a finger at the first page, pointing to the end of one of the letters that constituted most of the newspaper. "Does that say Mollie Lehman? Sam says it doesn't, but he doesn't know how to read, ain't so? I said it looks like the name she writes on the board at school. Is that our Mollie's name, *Daed*?"

When she paused to take a breath, he asked a question of his own. "May I see it?"

"Ja." She tapped the page again. "See? Isn't that our Mollie's name?"

Our Mollie. He hadn't heard her use that term before, and he wasn't certain how he felt about it. On one hand, he was glad the *kinder* had welcomed her into their lives, but at the same time, it made him uneasy. He wasn't sure why. He didn't like being dubious about anything or anyone where his *kinder* were concerned.

He took the paper and scanned the columns. His breath

caught when he saw the letter that began with the words *Lost River, Colorado*. It ended with Mollie's name. As he read the letter that was about a third of the column in length, he wondered if he'd made another huge mistake by not learning more about Mollie Lehman before hiring her.

Holding the small dress over the top of the washing machine, Mollie frowned. She'd scrubbed the polyester by hand, working to get paint splotches off the dark green fabric. She'd missed several. They were bright white. How Angela had gotten white paint on her dress when the *kinder* weren't supposed to touch Noah's painting supplies was a mystery neither kid could explain.

Mollie glanced out of the laundry room behind the bunkhouse's kitchen. Both youngsters were at the table coloring the pages she'd brought with them. Noah hadn't been in the locked studio when they arrived home, so she'd brought the kids into the house. When she'd seen stacks of dirty clothes, she decided to do laundry.

She set aside the splattered dress and reached for the other clothing inside the washer. It was a fancy front-loader with more lights and controls than she could have imagined any one machine possessing. She'd needed Angela's help in figuring out how to make it run. The little girl had seen a similar machine in Wisconsin.

The damp clothes went into the dryer. After closing the door, she touched the panel to start it, and hoped she was doing it correctly. She smiled as the clothing tumbled. It was a nice break from having to hang everything on the line and having to pray that no birds would dirty on them before they dried. On the other hand, she missed the fresh scent that billowed from clothing dried outside.

As she rubbed paint speckles from the dress, resorting

to using her nails to break them free of the fabric, she wondered when Noah did laundry. The noise from the washer and dryer, though muted compared with the diesel-powered washing machine in the lean-to at her family's home, would disrupt the *kinder*'s sleep.

She looked at the stacks of clothes waiting on the floor and wondered *if* he did laundry. She put another load of clothing into the washer, then added the little dress after she'd loosened all the paint attached to the polyester.

Mollie came into the great room and was about to check on the *kinder* when the door opened. Her heart did a silly leap at the moment she realized it was Noah. She tried to ignore it. Noah saw her as his *kinder*'s teacher and their nanny. That was for the best because he was a man who loved having a family, and she couldn't give him one.

Why had *that* thought appeared in her head? He'd never given her the slightest suggestion he was interested in her as anything other than an employee.

Her smile wavered as he regarded her with what appeared to be unconcealed anger, but she said, "When you weren't home, I brought Sam and Angela inside to color. I assumed that would be okay. Did your meeting go well?"

He didn't answer as he walked to the table by the sofa and picked up a newspaper. "I want to talk to you about this."

"*The Budget*? What about it?"

"Not the whole paper. Just this one page."

"Which page?" She held out her hand for it.

Instead of handing it to her, he said, "It starts with 'Lost River, Colorado. May is a month—'"

"You don't need to read it aloud. I know what I wrote."

He acted as if he hadn't heard her as he began over again.

"'Lost River, Colorado—May is a month when God's glorious palette is on full display here in our valley. The glorious greens of the trees in the mountains are the backdrop for our fields and barns. Potatoes have been planted, and our gardens have, too, as we envision the jars of vegetables that will be stored in our cellars come fall. The women of our district enjoyed a quilting day at our house earlier this week. With their generosity of time and skill, we'll be donating three quilts this summer to auctions. One to the fire department, one to the ambulance service and the last to the school.'

"'We must keep an eye on our gardens, though. Low temperatures have reached to freezing two nights in the past week. We know summer is on its way, a reason for planning picnics and fishing and grilling.'

"'A son born to the LaWayne Yoders was sent to a hospital in Denver for heart surgery. It's expected they'll be there for at least a month. Let's shower this family with cards.'

"'The Raymond Bylers have journeyed to Sugarcreek, Ohio, to spend time with family. The Aden Eichers are on their way to Jamesport, Missouri, for the wedding of Aden's younger sister.'

"'A meeting for local schoolteachers to share ideas for the new school year will be held the third Saturday of June at the home of Mollie Lehman. Teachers in the area are invited to attend.'

"'We welcomed newcomers, the Vernon Rennos and Emma Weaver, at this week's church. They've migrated from Ohio and Indiana.'"

He lowered the paper. "Do you always go into such detail about other people's business in your letters in *The Budget*?"

"Of course." She gave him the frown she reserved for a recalcitrant scholar who refused to study. "That's why people read the paper. To find out what their friends and relatives in other communities are doing. It's a *gut* way to keep track of everyone."

"Even those who might not want to be kept track of?" His lips grew taut.

Shocked, she stared at him. Never had she considered that someone might want to stay out of sight. Most people enjoyed seeing their names or their family's names in the newspaper.

"Noah, I won't mention you and your *kinder* if that's what you prefer."

"It is."

She hesitated, then realized she couldn't let the conversation end like that. "Are you and your family in trouble?"

He pressed the newspaper into her hand. "I get more than my share of publicity for working on barn-quilt trails. I'm not looking for more." He motioned to Angela and Sam. "Ready to head out to the studio?"

As he walked out with his *kinder*, Mollie didn't move. He hadn't answered her question.

What was he hiding?

Chapter Six

Mollie smiled at her scholars before glancing around her classroom on the last school day of the year. It was filled with adults as well as *kinder* too young to attend school. She couldn't help noticing how Noah stood in the corner by the front window on the right.

Alone.

Other parents smiled in his direction or spoke a greeting, and he replied in kind, but each motion, each word, pointed out he was there by himself. Why was Noah so determined to keep himself and his son and daughter separate? The plain people lived apart from the rest of the world, but not from each other. They joined together in a church community that supported one another in *gut* times and bad.

Yet, Noah wanted none of that. Was it the reason why he traveled from one part of the country to another, never putting down roots? She couldn't imagine a life like that. Her family had been in the San Luis Valley for two generations, and she had no plans to leave the high flatland, with its protective triangle of mountain ranges surrounding it.

"When are we starting?" whispered one of the scholars.

She didn't catch who'd spoken, but she returned her attention to them. Now wasn't the time to let her thoughts drift. The *kinder* had worked too hard to have the program ruined by her distraction.

"Take a deep breath," Mollie urged the scholars. "Be calm, because you have practiced and practiced this program. You can do your best."

She needed to take the same advice for herself.

This was the sixth end-of-the-year presentation she'd done since she finished with her own school years in this building. The first two years, she'd been an assistant teacher, but for the past four end-of-year presentations, she'd been the only teacher. So why did she feel as if a cloud of butterflies bounced inside her?

Because Noah is here this year, came the answer from inside her.

She didn't want to heed that practical voice, so she said, "Let's take another deep breath." The request was more for herself than the scholars. She didn't want anyone to see her fingers trembling when she pointed to each *kind* to indicate it was his or her turn to step forward.

She glanced over her shoulder again. The single room felt too small, though it was larger than many of the houses where they held church services. Families crowded around the desks and everywhere they could have a *gut* view of the participants.

A pair of intense eyes caught her gaze. Noah's. She tried to look away, but couldn't. Their powerful emotions teased her to try to discover what was behind his request to write nothing for *The Budget* about his visit to the valley.

"Teacher Mollie?" a voice whispered. "Can't we sing?"

This time, she recognized the voice. It belonged to Sam.

"*Gut* things *komm* to those who wait." She smiled, though it wasn't easy. Again, it was advice she could use more than the scholars. "Are you ready?"

The hearty response of *"Ja!"* brought silence from the rest of the room because the families, including her former scholars, knew that question meant the end-of-the-year presentation was about to begin.

As she motioned for the *kinder* to take their places on the raised platform where her desk sat, she waited to join them. Her eyes wanted to shift to where Noah stood, but she kept her gaze on the scholars. They *had* worked hard, and they deserved every bit of her attention. She hoped she could give it to them.

Noah felt like a pretender. An outsider who shouldn't have been there. The other parents had been involved through the whole school year. Some for many years. Angela and Sam had been attending the school for less than ten days. Yet, Mollie had insisted they should take part in the end-of-year program and that he should join the other parents at the presentation.

"They've made friends among the scholars," Mollie had said in her no-nonsense teacher voice. "They must participate in the program."

"All right," he'd agreed.

"You must attend."

That had surprised him, and he'd asked in a voice almost as high as his son's, "Me? Why? I don't know any of the other parents."

"This will be a *gut* opportunity for you to meet them and the scholars, so you'll be able to put a face with a name when Sam and Angela talk about their new friends."

It'd made complete sense then, but he should have listened to his instincts that he'd stick out like a splash of bright red paint. He'd been right because he saw the surreptitious, curious glances. He'd spent more time with the arts commission's members than with plain folks in the valley. On Sunday, he would worship for the first time with them. He'd linger after the service because he'd promised Mollie that he would allow his *kinder* an hour or two to play basketball with the kids. He'd have a chance to meet his neighbors, but he hoped it wouldn't give them time to grill him about why his family was incomplete. So far, he'd been able to truncate any conversation and avoid that topic. He was grateful that *gut* manners had halted the questions.

Just as being polite had kept Mollie from quizzing him about why he was averse to having his name or his *kinder*'s name in the newspaper. He doubted she could guess the reason behind his request. She didn't know—nobody but he did—how determined he was to keep his in-laws from learning where he, Angela and Sam were. Yet, somehow, he sensed she'd found him lacking.

Why shouldn't she? He found himself lacking. If he'd been there when the fire started, he'd be home now in Lancaster County, raising Angela and Sam with their *mamm*. He wouldn't have to be worried old friends or family would discover where he and the *kinder* were. Mollie couldn't imagine hiding from the rest of the world because she was comfortable in her community. She couldn't conceive of a family that wasn't like hers.

Noah heard Mollie ask if the scholars were ready. It must have been a signal for the event to get underway. He rested his shoulder on the wall next to a collection of posters created by the youngsters about spring flowers. Settling his thumbs into his pockets, he watched the *kinder* take their places.

As they grinned and squirmed with anticipation and anxiety, he remembered his own programs at the end of each school year. He'd been the tallest boy by the time he was ten, so he'd been assigned to the rear. He was surprised Sam stood in the second row, though he was the youngest. He hadn't realized how his son had sprouted up in the past year.

The presentation was simple, starting with a prayer and a one of their favorite hymns as each school day would have. Then the scholars had their turn to recite, beginning with Sam as the youngest.

Noah held his breath, hoping his son would do well. As Sam began, Noah discovered he hadn't needed to worry. The poem was simple, and Sam's voice was steady and clear. His fingers matched the motions of a little bird awakening in its nest and taking its first flight. When he spoke of how it nearly tumbled from the sky and then found its way among the clouds, there wasn't another sound in the room.

Applause followed, and plenty of smiles were aimed in Noah's direction. He nodded to the other parents and made sure he returned those smiles as their *kinder* stepped forward, one or two at a time, to recite. It was easy to tell which parents belonged to which scholar because their expressions became first anxious, then relieved, then pleased as the *kind* finished his or her presentation.

Angela stepped forward with two girls who looked close to her age. The three of them sang a song about a pair of puppies and a kitten, each girl taking on one role. Angela's voice as one of the dogs rang through the room. Laughter from the parents created a deeper undertone to their song, and the little girls blushed with delight when they were finished.

The two girls moved back, but Angela remained where she was. Her whole demeanor changed as she began to recite a poem about the first lamb born one year. The lamb felt lost among the older sheep until more lambs began to appear, including a set of triplets. The little creature had been so happy to have playmates she'd been willing to share her *mamm*'s milk with one of the triplets whose own ewe didn't have enough.

Noah was shocked when tears pricked at his eyes. Something in his daughter's heartfelt recitation was so genuine he couldn't help wondering if Angela was speaking of herself and her brother instead of the two lambs. The lamb that had longed for playmates and the lamb whose *mamm* couldn't care for her.

That thought stayed with him through the whole presentation. He applauded when the rest did and tried to laugh along, but he couldn't shake the idea that the poem had expressed Angela's true feelings. Had she chosen it, or had Mollie selected it for her?

It took almost an hour before he could find a moment to speak to Mollie alone. As most of the scholars and their families were packing up after the picnic and were leaving, he espied Mollie go into the schoolhouse. She opened the closet and pulled out the broom. She was going to give the room its last cleaning until the school reopened in the fall.

Would he and his kids be here then? It would depend on what the ongoing support was for the barn-quilts trail project. He didn't want to think about that because he didn't have any further work lined up.

"Did you enjoy the presentation, Noah?" Mollie asked, and he realized he'd walked into the school while lost in his uncomfortable musings.

Shaking aside those thoughts, he said, "I did."

"Your *kinder* worked hard to accomplish a lot in a short time."

"I was astonished, to be honest. I had no idea what they were going to do."

She paused in her sweeping. "Didn't you hear them practicing?"

He shook his head. "Not once."

"They told me they were practicing every evening at home."

Not wanting to admit he'd fallen asleep two of the past three nights after supper, he didn't want to complain about his long days of being driven from one end of the valley to the other so he could appraise barns that would be adorned with the barn quilts. She worked as hard as he did.

"I'm sure they wanted to surprise me," he said. "They succeeded."

"I'm glad you're pleased."

"You spent a lot of time on this program."

"The kids love it, and so do the families. It's *gut* you decided to *komm*. Several of the parents wanted to meet you. The Rupps and the Yoders, especially, because their *kinder* helped get Angela and Sam settled in at school. Did you have a chance to speak with them?"

"I may have. Lots of folks said hello, but I didn't catch everyone's name." If he said he'd been too unsettled by Angela's recitation, Mollie might have thought that was silly. Maybe it was, but he couldn't change the past.

That was something he knew for certain because if he could have, he would have done so five years ago.

Walking into his studio two afternoons later after an interminable meeting at the visitors' center in downtown Lost River, Noah stopped in midstep. What had happened? Nothing was where it should have been, but nothing appeared to be missing. Just not where he'd left it. The corner where his *kinder* played had been decorated with a pair of well-worn quilts on the floor.

Short arms were thrown around his legs, and he looked at Angela's big grin. "Do you like it, *Daed*?"

"I'm not sure what to think." He was about to add more when Mollie walked in with his son and their host.

The sunlight turned Mollie's hair to burnished gold, but its glow couldn't compare to the sparkle in her eyes, which were the rich color of a cloudless sky. In a pale blue dress with a black apron and with her white *kapp*, she looked so lovely that he wished he could paint her portrait. No plain woman would pose like that, but he imagined what shades he would use to bring to life her warm, pink cheeks and the gentle arch of her eyebrows. Even her scars would be intriguing to recreate.

He again banished his thoughts as he saw her widening smile. "Do you know what happened in here, Mollie?"

"*Ja*. We—"

"We fixed it!" Sam announced, bouncing from one foot to the other before running forward and throwing his arms around Noah's other leg. "Don't you love it, *Daed*?"

"Do you, *Daed*?" echoed Angela. "We worked hard to get it right."

He looked at Mollie and Carlos for clarification.

"You mentioned that the light was wrong in here," she said, "so I spoke yesterday with Carlos."

"I had my men help move things to where Mollie said you'd want it," the older man said.

Mollie added, "Angela and Sam helped."

"We didn't touch your paints, *Daed*," Angela quickly added. "We made sure nobody did."

A pulse of guilt raced through him. He couldn't count the number of times he'd warned his *kinder* to stay away from the cans.

He walked to where the sawhorses sat within the beam of light from the window that offered a northern exposure. It was the perfect light, clear and colorless, for seeing as he painted, so he could tell what the barn quilt would look like once it was hung.

"*Danki*." He turned to include his host in his smile. "This should work well. I didn't expect this."

"Which," Carlos said with a chuckle, "was why we were glad to do it when Mollie asked for our help." He winked at her, then clapped Noah on the back. "Now, you can produce those barn quilts for us."

"If I can get time to paint instead of playing mediator in these battles at every meeting."

Carlos's dark eyebrows lowered, giving him a forbidding expression, as he said with a feigned growl, "I was wondering how long you'd endure the prattle. Let me handle the arts commission. You paint." He motioned to the *kinder.* "C'mon. Lynny left her famous chili brownies on the counter. If there are any left when she gets home, she'll be upset. She'll be upset, too, if she thinks I ate them all. Will you help me stay out of trouble?"

His son and daughter looked to him for permission, and he hesitated.

"I'll bring them outside, so we can eat them on the steps," Carlos added with a glance in Mollie's direction. "If you work hard, Noah, we may save you one."

Startled at how easily and accurately Carlos had sensed his unease, Noah nodded. The *kinder* didn't wait on the chance he might change his mind. They ran toward the main house.

"I won't let them near any horses," his host said before turning to follow the kids. "For their sake and for my horses' sakes."

When Mollie started to leave as well, he said, "A moment, please."

"What is it?"

He closed the distance between them with a pair of steps. He noticed the pale shadows that accented the curves of her face. Painting her might be impossible, but he doubted he'd forget her face. Not because of her scars. He'd remember because her features were alive with every emotion that spiraled through her.

"I wanted to say *danki* to you, too, for getting Carlos and his men to make these changes. I know I've been lamenting how it's been impossible to paint, but I hadn't guessed I was complaining about the space and the light here."

"It wasn't complaining as much as hearing you talk to Angela and Sam about how you missed your studio in Wisconsin, which had such a *wunderbaar* window to let in the northern light." She gestured toward the rear of the barn. "This building has great potential, too, so I figured we'd give you a nice surprise by shifting everything to its best advantage."

He couldn't find words. She wasn't a painter. Yet, somehow, she'd been able to see the stable as if looking through his eyes. Her insight was remarkable. Though he knew he should be worried what else she might have perceived, he was grateful to be able to live in this exceptional moment when he could push his past into the past for a few seconds.

Only a few, though, because guilt would soon return to drown him in its dark, serrated depths. There was nothing he could do to halt it.

Mollie couldn't help but notice how Noah abruptly pulled within himself, as if he'd been beaten. Nobody had touched him other than his *kinder*'s enthusiastic greeting. His gaze grew dull, and she wondered where his thoughts were.

"Have you decided which barn quilt you're going to work on first, Noah?"

"*Ja.*"

She had to figure out a way to pull him out of his grim mood. She needed to convince him to give her more than a one-word answer. Hoping she wasn't pushing too hard, she asked, "Will you share what you're going to be working on, or do you prefer to wait until it's finished? *Mamm* likes to keep her special cakes to herself until she's satisfied."

"No, I don't mind sharing along the way." He motioned for her to follow him to a file folder that still sat on the plywood table. Opening it, he pulled out a slip of paper and set it on the board across the sawhorses. "This is my sketch for the first one."

She'd expected something simple. A few lines drawn by a pencil. Instead, it was an intricate pattern done with colored pencils. It would have made a stunning quilt, with its dark background and flowers in shades of lavender and white.

"Columbines," she breathed. "How perfect for the first quilt. Our state flower, and they grow in the valley where the ground is marshy."

He got a pack of colored pencils from one of the pails. They flew over the board, outlining a simple design of more flowers rising from the ground. Behind them, aspen trees took shape with a few quick strokes. He edged the central pattern with a border, where he sketched in a few of the local birds, including the sandhill cranes that migrated through the San Luis Valley in February and September.

"Are these the actual colors you'll be using?" she asked in little more than a whisper.

"*Ja*. I'm using a blue-purple for the columbines. As you can see, the aspen leaves will be yellow." He gave her a wry smile. "I know that's depicting two different seasons, summer and fall, but those colors will draw the eye toward the quilt. The red on the head of the sandhill crane and the wing of the white-faced ibis will contrast with the iridescent blue of the mountain bluebird. I've got two of each bird along the border." He put the pencils down and faced her. "This barn quilt will hang on the town barn behind the visitors' information center. It's meant to be the beginning of the initial barn-quilt trail, though that may change if other counties get involved."

"It's going to be lovely."

"I hope so."

"I *know* so. God has given you an amazing talent."

"He's given you an amazing talent, too."

She shook her head. "What talent do I have? Not writing. It doesn't take any skill to throw the local news together and send it off to *The Budget*."

The wrong thing to say, she feared. Neither of them had mentioned the newspaper since he'd insisted she say nothing of him or the *kinder* in any of her upcoming letters.

When he answered, she released a breath she'd been holding because he didn't speak about the newspaper. "Mollie, don't sell yourself short. You've got a talent for reaching into young minds and implanting knowledge. I'm amazed at how Angela was able to recite that long poem when she was with you for such a short time."

"She's eager to learn. I'd offered her a simpler poem, but she insisted on doing something more."

"She takes after her *mamm* in that. Betty Jane always tried to challenge herself, whether it was baking a new sort of cake or adding something different to her pickles."

She gasped.

"What is it?" he asked.

"You mentioned your wife." She couldn't keep her voice from trembling as she picked her words with care. "That's the first time I've heard you say her name."

"I don't like to talk about her in front of the kids."

"Why?"

He gawped at her. "What do you mean?"

"I mean if you're trying to spare them from pain and grief, you're wasting your time. They're sad whenever they think about her. I've seen that when the other *kinder* talk about their families."

"Time is passing. They'll come to understand why I don't say much."

"Because time cures grief? How's that working out for you?" She clamped her hand over her mouth, then lowered it. "I'm sorry, Noah. I shouldn't have said that."

"No, you shouldn't have, but you're right. When people told me I'd come to terms with Betty Jane's death, I wanted to believe them. You've got no idea how much I wanted to believe them, but nothing they said was true. Time doesn't heal every wound, especially when her death could have been prevented."

She couldn't imagine that Noah wouldn't do everything possible to make sure his wife got the best care possible. She knew sometimes top-of-the-line care wasn't enough because her *daed* had died in spite of the Herculean efforts of his *doktors* and the rest of the medical staffs at the hospitals where he was sent for surgery and chemo. "Was she ill?"

"No, she died in a fire. Betty Jane's *mamm*, Jane, and the *kinder* escaped. Betty Jane did not. If I'd been there, the outcome would have been different."

"You can't know that for sure."

"I do." He turned on his heel and walked out of the studio before she said another word.

She stared after him. No wonder he was so exacting about having his *kinder* with him. She'd heard the term "haunted by the past," but she doubted she'd understood it until now. While she would have given almost anything to reclaim her lost memories of the night she was injured, Noah was desperate to escape his.

Chapter Seven

The church service was much like ones Noah had attended in Pennsylvania and in Ohio and in Indiana and in Illinois and in Wisconsin. Though the faces and voices were different, if he'd closed his eyes, he could have been in any of those places where the *Leit* came together on a Sunday morning to worship and praise God together.

He went through the motions of kneeling and rising and singing and listening to the sermons as he had each church Sunday. In the weeks after Betty Jane's funeral, he'd avoided services because his anger had roiled harder when he was among those who accepted God's will.

He couldn't.

His eyes shifted toward Mollie. From where he sat, he couldn't see the scars on her pretty face. It wasn't necessary. Her face appeared with ease in his mind whenever he wanted it to. Even when he didn't, because he'd found himself focusing more on her features than his painting. That she'd been so excited about the design for his first barn quilt for the San Luis Valley had added speed and precision to his brush. He couldn't wait to show her the barn quilt when the two pieces were finished and put together.

How could she accept God's will that she should be injured and left with those eye-drawing scars? The wounds must have changed her life, just as Betty Jane's death had altered his. Yet, he'd seen no sign of her doubting God's love. She sang with obvious delight and smiled as she whispered to Angela when they kneeled beside the pews before one of the ministers led them in prayer.

He continued to ponder those puzzles through the long service, becoming so lost in thought he missed the cue to stand and sing until the men on either side of him elbowed him at the same time. Scrambling to his feet, he hoped nobody believed he'd fallen asleep. That wasn't a *gut* way to make a first impression on the *Leit*.

He realized he didn't need to worry because the men had to shake one of their own awake. The man looked sheepish as he yawned. The long hours of a farmer's day left too little time for sleep. The group didn't tease the man then, or later, when they gathered for the after-worship meal. Apparently, someone falling asleep wasn't unusual.

The men were welcoming, asking about how his work was going, but Noah couldn't shake off the feeling of being an outsider when they spoke of people he hadn't met and events he had no knowledge of. It wasn't like they were trying to exclude him. Quite the contrary. He appreciated their efforts, and didn't remind them he'd be in the community only until he finished the barn quilts.

As soon as he could excuse himself, Noah did. After making sure his kids were being supervised while they played basketball, he wandered around the farm and marveled at the long, straight rows of potato hills, which would be harvested in the late summer. They were a lush green beneath giant, spidery irrigation pumps.

He remained by a fence, though he should have returned. It wasn't polite to shrug off the welcome he'd received, but he wasn't comfortable being the center of attention while his neighbors tried to convince him to talk more about himself.

That was something he'd never do. What would they think of the man who had failed to save his wife? The burns left after he'd attempted to enter the house and been driven back by flames and smoke had healed. The invisible scars were as raw and painful as the day Betty Jane had died.

Noah sensed rather than heard someone behind him, shattering the self-loathing that was his constant companion. The same nameless sense told him the person approaching was Mollie. He glanced over his shoulder to see her smile, and the feeling he didn't belong there—or anywhere else—diminished.

"I thought I might find you out here." Her words, as she folded her arms on the fence pole near where he stood, weren't an accusation. He knew he'd been rude to desert the rest of the gathering to seek a perfect solitude. Instead, he heard her empathy when she added, "I like to find a few minutes alone, too, on a church Sunday. It's *wunderbaar* to worship with others, but sometimes I seek God on my own. Am I disturbing your prayers?"

He shook his head, not trusting his voice. His solitude by the fence hadn't been perfect. It'd been familiar. The familiarity of loneliness and guilt and wishing he could change what was forever unchangeable.

"I'm admiring the view," he said, glad he sounded calm.

"Isn't it stunning? I love how we're surrounded by mountains. It's as if we're *bopplin* tucked into a cozy triangular cradle." She gave him another smile. "A cradle a hundred miles long and more than sixty miles wide."

He whistled under his breath, not because of the information she was sharing, but at how she was able to pull him out of his doldrums with her warm smile. "I didn't realize that. Those mountains to the west must be higher than I thought."

"There are more than a dozen fourteeners—mountains with elevations over fourteen thousand feet—in the San Juan Mountains alone."

His eyebrows rose. "I can see why you're a schoolteacher. You've got those facts at your fingertips."

"It has more to do with a brother who loves skiing. Tyler grabs on to any excuse to go into the San Juans for back-country skiing."

"I haven't met your brother."

"I've got two. Tyler is the oldest and Kolton is next. I'm the last, as they've reminded me for as long as I can remember." She arched her eyebrows, as he had. "I've spent my whole life trying to keep up with them."

"Do you ski, too?"

"No. I prefer to admire the mountains from their bases." She drew in a deep breath of the fresh air. "The peaks are so roughhewn it's as if we're able to watch God raise them right in front of us. Everything feels new and old at the same time."

"I heard Angela say that last night before bed."

Her smile softened as it did when she spoke of her scholars. "I try to teach them to open their eyes and exult in the astounding world around them. For *kinder*, God may be too big for them to comprehend, but they can understand the beauty of a mountain or the expanse of the sky or the thrill of seeing birds overhead."

"You inspire your students."

"That's a teacher's job. Not just teaching rote facts, like the alphabet and multiplication tables. I'll have done my job if I can lead them to see how God has given us minds to learn and hearts to fill with the desire to discover more about His gifts to us." She wrinkled her nose. "You don't have to be so nice and let me prattle on and on and on."

"You listen to me prattle on and on and on about my painting. Why should your passion for teaching be any less interesting?"

"Because anyone can—"

He put his finger to her lips, silencing her. Astonished, he knew he shouldn't have been so bold, but his arm refused to move his hand from her soft skin. Instead, his fingertips pleaded with him to let them explore her face and tilt it toward his so he could taste her lips. If he did, it would alter everything, but he couldn't let that happen when the past remained carved in stone. And that stone had his wife's name on it in a plain cemetery in Pennsylvania. Yet one kiss would be so *wunderbaar...*

Looking into Noah's face, Mollie saw the conflicting emotions racing through his eyes. Did they match the ones within her? The motion of touching someone else's lips, which she'd often used to quiet a scholar, was far from commonplace when it was *his* finger against *her* lips. Delightful sensations danced through her. Sensations she shouldn't be feeling for her employer. He didn't know the truth about the appalling legacy of the accident and the *doktor*'s belief she could never give birth to a *boppli*. Noah adored his *kinder*, and she had no doubts he'd love to have more.

The words of the one hundred and twenty-seventh Psalm played through her head: *Lo, children are an heritage of the Lord: and the fruit of the womb is His reward. As arrows are in the hand of a mighty man; so are children of the youth.*

Happy is the man that hath his quiver full of them. Every plain man held those verses close to his heart.

Mollie reminded herself of that throughout Sunday and on

Monday. The thoughts loitered in her head when she walked down the road after supper to attend a quilting gathering at the Geers' house. Ruthanne had been excited yesterday about being able to host the twice-monthly meeting at her house. The last time it'd been her turn had been the day her *mamm* announced she was heading east to attend her *kinskind*'s birth. That had thrown the whole family into chaos.

Mollie had decided not to join them tonight, because she'd figured she wouldn't be *gut* company, but *Mamm* had pushed her to go. Was it because *Mamm* wanted the house to herself tonight? Mollie's brothers were busy elsewhere—Tyler at the store and Kolton at the fire department, where he'd recently finished his training as a volunteer.

Would *Mamm* be alone? Howard Zehr's name had been on her *mamm*'s lips often, and Mollie couldn't fail to notice how her *mamm*'s voice became lighter with each mention of their neighbor's name. Howard had been a *gut* friend to her parents, and Mollie was glad he was remaining in her *mamm*'s life.

The door opened before Mollie could reach for the knob.

"I wasn't sure if you'd be here," Ruthanne said as she swung the door wider. "You've been busy with the Frye *kinder*."

"Time goes fast when I'm enjoying myself."

Carrie Detweiler giggled as she walked past. "I'm sure you are. Noah Frye is a fine-looking man."

Mollie glanced at Ruthanne, who rolled her eyes. Carrie was the youngest in their circle by almost three years. She wouldn't be twenty for several months. As tall as her brother, Gerald, who was a year older, there was nothing masculine about the statuesque blonde. Her cheeks were a delightful pink, and her bright green eyes twinkled. Ruthanne had mentioned more than once that two of the younger brothers of Albert, her fiancé, were interested in driving Carrie home from youth events. Both had had their hopes dashed because Carrie was always escorted by her brother.

"That's the first time I've heard her talk about a guy being *gut*-looking," Ruthanne said when Carrie was out of earshot. "Our youngster is finally taking notice of the men around her."

Mollie laughed as she guessed her friend expected, but her thoughts were buzzing with ideas she couldn't have conceived of a moment ago.

Noah needed someone to watch his *kinder*. Not just watch them, but to raise them and love them. She could do two out of the three. She couldn't be a *mamm* to them because their *daed* deserved a wife who could give him more *bopplin*.

Carrie had been Mollie's assistant teacher before going to work as a waitress at the Central Valley Diner on the road to Alamosa. Mollie had seen her interact with the scholars, from the youngest to the oldest. Carrie had patience with *kinder* and found a way to make them giggle with her. She would be *wunderbaar* with Angela and Sam.

It was a simple solution, though thinking about it made her stomach twist. No, she couldn't think about herself. What she wanted was impossible, anyhow, so why not help Noah and his darling *kinder*?

As if Mollie had spoken aloud, Carrie paused in the hallway with a plate of ginger cookies and said, "If you need help with the *kinder*, I'd be glad to step in."

"That's generous of you. I know you're busy at home."

Carrie's nose wrinkled in an elfin grin. "Too busy at times. It'd be fun to spend my time with cute kids instead of my brother, who never remembers to wipe his feet. So if you need a day off to help your *mamm* or to do errands, let me know. I'll be more than happy to step in." Again, she grinned. "It'll be better to step in with the kids than what Gerald steps in the sheep barn and then brings into the house."

"*Danki* for offering. I may need your help during the teachers' meeting I'm hosting in a couple of weeks."

"Let me know when, and I'll be glad to take over for you." Her face became more animated. "I've never met a plain man who's an artist."

"He looks at his barn quilts the same way we look at our quilts."

"How? Our quilts are useful. A barn quilt is pretty, but not useful."

She set her cloth bag over her shoulder. "I don't agree. We make quilts to donate to the fire department or the ambulance service. The money they raise helps the community. It's the same with Noah's barn quilts. By creating a trail for tourists to follow, the barn quilts will bring new customers to small towns throughout the county."

"I never considered that." Carrie tilted her head like a puppy intrigued with a new toy. "You always give me something different to think about, Mollie. I learned so much from you when I was your assistant teacher. I miss that now."

Walking into the dining room while Carrie told amusing stories about the people she met at the diner, Mollie saw the table had been shoved against the wall between two tall windows. In its place, a large quilting frame claimed the center of the floor. It was flanked by chairs. On top of the table were baskets holding pincushions and spools of thread. Papers with needles stuck into them were arranged in front of the other supplies. In the corner, but within reach of the quilting frame, was a low, upholstered wing chair that had seen better times, but it was there in case someone, most often Idella Swantz, had a small *kind* with them. The little one could sit there and not get cookie crumbs too close to the quilt-in-progress.

Her eyes were drawn to the quilt top pinned to the frame, waiting for the beautiful seams that would attach it to the batting and bottom layer. She loved this pattern. It was a wedding-star quilt. The pieced fabric in purples, blues, greens and golds intersected with the patched circles that were more than a foot in diameter, and was more intricate than the more recognizable double-wedding-ring quilt.

Mollie greeted Idella, a usually spare woman who, despite being in her thirties, had streaks of gray in her black hair. Taking her seat across the frame from Idella, she asked about the other woman's six *kinder.* Idella was growing round with number seven, and she seldom missed a quilting session because she enjoyed the chance for adult female conversation.

When Ruthanne joined them, bringing iced tea, they began work. The other two members of their quilting circle weren't able to attend, so there was no reason to wait. Conversation centered on the newcomers to their community. Carrie had spoken to Emma Weaver after church, but hadn't learned much about the redhead who had a *boppli* that didn't look much older than two months old. Emma and her daughter had moved alone to Lost River, and Mollie guessed Emma was a widow, having lost her spouse too soon, as Noah had.

"Emma is a seamstress," Carrie said. "She's finding a lot of work among the *Englischers*."

"I wonder if she likes to quilt." Mollie dipped her needle into the fabric.

"I'll ask her the next time I see her."

"It'd be nice to have a *boppli* here," Idella said, "that isn't one of mine."

That brought laughter around the frame before Ruthanne shared she'd spent time getting to know Vernon and Eve Renno, who were newlyweds living with his cousins while they looked for a home of their own. "Vernon wants to get into solar installation, so he's working with a company in Lost River. That leaves your newcomers, Mollie. You've been spending a lot of time with the Frye family."

"Because I'm watching Angela and Sam." She made a silly face at her friend. "They're sweet *kinder*, though a bit mischievous like any their ages."

"And their *daed*?"

"Noah is excited about the barn-quilt-trail project. He's done similar projects in Wisconsin and Illinois. In Indiana as well."

"You know a lot about him, Mollie!"

Looking at the quilt, she almost said she hardly knew him because he kept so much to himself. That would prompt more curiosity from her friends, so she said, "You know how *kinder* are. A teacher hears more about their parents and families than she should. I've learned to put most of it out of my head because its accuracy is questionable."

That brought more laughter as well as more questions about the barn-quilt trail. When Mollie explained that Noah was going to need help in selecting patterns for the quilts, Ruthanne slipped her needle into the fabric so it wouldn't be lost.

"Let me see where *Mamm* put those books about southwestern quilts." Ruthanne stood. "They might be on her night table. She enjoys looking at them before she goes to sleep. Says they give her inspiration and pleasant dreams."

"If Noah could borrow them, that would be *wunder-*

baar." Mollie almost clapped her hands in glee. "I'll make sure he knows not to get any paint on them."

"I know I can trust a teacher with books." Ruthanne returned quickly. She dropped a stack of a half-dozen books on the overstuffed chair. "Enjoy them. *Mamm* won't be back until the week before..." She flushed.

Carrie rolled her eyes. "Don't act as if nobody knows you and Albert Wynes are going to have your wedding published soon. We've heard you and Mollie conspiring about it for weeks."

"Okay, okay." Ruthanne raised her hands in surrender. "Don't tell anyone else."

"We won't," Idella and Carrie said together before Idella added, "It's about time one of you *maedels* got married. You don't want to be left as the last apple on the tree, ain't so?"

Mollie let her friends joke with each other, saying enough so they didn't notice she'd lost her smile. She hated that old saying. She knew who would be the last apple—or unmarried woman—among her friends in Lost River.

Mollie Lehman. The woman every man considered a friend, but the woman none had any interest in walking out with since her disfiguring accident.

Did Noah think of her that way, too? If so, why had he gazed intently at her after church yesterday?

She told herself to stop being fanciful. Noah still mourned his wife. His *kinder* enjoyed spending time with her, but that didn't mean they wanted her to step in and take their *mamm*'s place.

She was better off leaving things as they were. She had a loving family and dear friends and a job she couldn't wait to get to each day of the school year. That should have been enough for her.

But she wasn't sure it was any longer.

Chapter Eight

The following morning, Mollie took Sam and Angela with her to the school building so she could store and clean everything. The quick sweep she'd done on the day of the end-of-the-year presentation wasn't enough. Dust blew in and seeped past any loose joint in the building to gather on the floor.

The *kinder* had been disappointed they were the only scholars there, though she'd warned them the others were at home, helping their families with chores of their own. Soon, both youngsters were stacking textbooks on shelves.

She'd planned to use the time to get Noah's kids out of his studio so he could have uninterrupted time for painting, and she hadn't been certain if he'd agree to have Angela and Sam so far from his sight. When Carlos had popped his head around the door to give Noah the unwelcome news that there was another meeting planned for that morning, she'd known it was her opportunity to go to school and finish up there.

Mollie hummed and sang along with the *kinder* as she cleared out her desk and the scholars'. Some preferred to stuff trash in their desks rather than put it in the wastebasket. She dumped used practice pages, candy wrappers and sandwich bags into the large bin behind the school.

Two hours later, she'd gathered the materials she wanted to take home for the teachers' summer meeting, as well as information on the valley she thought Noah might find interesting. Squeezing the papers into her overloaded canvas bag, she grimaced. She should have given Noah the books borrowed from Ruthanne's *mamm*, but hadn't had a chance before he was called away.

She tied her black bonnet over her *kapp* and slung the bag's strap onto her shoulder. She asked the *kinder*, "Shall we head to the ranch and get some lemonade?"

"Ja!" they cheered, then turned toward the door. *"Daed!"*

"What are you doing here, Noah?" She realized how off-putting her question sounded. "How did your meeting go?"

He took off his straw hat as he entered and wiped his nape with a kerchief. "Not well. This one was about the second barn-quilt location."

"Where's it going to be?"

"Well, I should have said the *probable* second barn-quilt location because that was the biggest point of contention. Two businesses are vying to be the next in line. One in town, and the other is a farm near the nature reserve. The guy who owns the farm was upset when he saw sandhill cranes on the design for the barn quilt for the visitors' center. He thought he should have them on *his* barn quilt because the cranes were his neighbors on their stopover in the valley during the spring and fall migrations."

Mollie resisted rolling her eyes as if she was no older than Angela. "Certainly you're going to repeat motifs."

He put his hat on and doffed it toward her. *"Danki* for being sensible. You've got no idea how little common sense there is when people feel their opinion is the only one worthy of being heard."

"I thought Carlos was going to put an end to these meetings."

"He tried, and if it weren't for him, I'd still be stuck between two people arguing whether the third barn quilt should copy a real quilt design or if it should be something original. That was the other argument that overtook the meeting."

She crossed the schoolroom, motioning for the *kinder* to follow. "Aren't you the one who's supposed to design the quilts?"

"When I took on this commission, I was told to work with each property owner to design a pattern that suits them and their business." He shrugged. "Someone needs to tell them to work with me. Enough about that. Can I carry that bag for you? It looks heavy."

"It is, but I'm used to it." She adjusted the strap so it didn't dig into her.

"You don't make it easy to help. Are you always stubborn?"

"Always."

He grinned, looking as young and carefree as his son. There was something charming about the dimple in his left cheek. Was this what he'd been like before tragedy had changed him? Fun and funny and with a smile that held a woman's eyes?

Mollie looked away as the kids rushed out the door.

When Noah went after them, he held the door open for her. "That I'm supposed to be in charge of designing the barn quilts has flown out the window. I left everyone squabbling."

"What did the owner want for the third building?" she asked, knowing he needed to vent.

Who else did he have to talk to? Carlos was busy with his ranch, and Noah couldn't talk to the art commissioners. They were the problem. She hadn't realized until this moment how alone Noah was. Was that what he wanted? When she thought about him standing alone by the fence after church, she might have almost believed he did...except he'd been pleased to have her join him. He needed someone to share his life. If he and Carrie…

She couldn't finish that thought. Introducing them would be *gut*, but her heart was arguing it would be the worst thing she could do. She had to think of what was best for Noah, Angela and Sam. *Think of God first and then others and then yourself.* How many times had she told her scholars that? She needed to learn that lesson, too.

"I don't know what the owner thought," Noah said with a sigh as his youngsters ran for a final ride on the swings. "I never met her. The two going toe-to-toe were art commissioners. The chairman, Brant, and his vice chair, Wendy. I'm not sure why they try to convince everyone they're a team. As far as I can see, they take pride in being on the opposite side of every issue. Bureaucracy can suck the life out of a project like this one. I'm grateful Carlos stepped in and suggested the debate be continued over nachos at his favorite *taqueria*. He pulled me aside and told me to get going while the getting was *gut*. I owe him one for this."

"Join the club." She locked the door of the schoolhouse. The school board had asked her to keep the building secured during summer break. "Carlos and *Doktor* Lynny do so much for everyone in Lost River."

When she turned toward her lean-to, where her horse and buggy waited, Noah asked, "Can you leave Chester here?"

"I can, but why?"

"When I realized I'd be driving by the school, I figured I'd stop for the kids. I've told them I'd take them into Lost River when I had the chance. I figured today was as *gut* a day as any because my brain is so full of costs and marketing plans I don't have a single creative thought in my head." He glanced toward the empty road that was an unwavering straight line from the eastern horizon to the western. "Is there a place to get a soda or ice cream?"

"*Ja.* There's an ice-cream shop called The Shivering Banana. Their specialty is a huge banana split."

"Banana splits?" he asked, raising his voice so Angela and Sam couldn't fail to hear him. They jumped out of the swings and raced to him. "Sounds great, ain't so? Do you want to join us, Mollie?"

"How can I say no to ice cream?"

With a grin, he took her bag and put it in the back of the wagon. He lifted the kids into the bed before holding his hand out to Mollie.

Though she knew he intended to help her onto the wagon's seat, she couldn't bear the idea of letting this be the only time he touched her. The memory would haunt her for the rest of her days as a *maedel*. Not giving herself time for second thoughts, she scrambled onto the seat as if she hadn't noticed his outstretched fingers.

On the drive into Lost River, she kept up a steady conversation with the *kinder*, but she couldn't be unaware of the silent man handling the reins. She hadn't meant to hurt him. She wanted to protect her heart.

No, that wasn't the only thing she wanted…and that was the problem.

Noah had been in Lost River for many meetings, but he'd always arrived in Carlos's truck. Driving along the three blocks of the wide main street in the wagon gave him a chance to look around. The town, like so much else in the valley, was a square. Three blocks west and east, where a railroad line cut across the streets. Three blocks north and south, where more railroad lines marked the lower edge of the business district. Schools, a small medical center and scattered businesses were set amid small houses in a variety of colors.

A few vehicles—mostly pickup trucks—moved around the wagon. The buildings on either side were a variety of heights. The Lost River Motel at the far end of Main Street was the tallest at three stories. It was set across from the town barn, where the first barn quilt would be hung.

People paused to chat or look in the windows that weren't covered with kraft paper and signs announcing a new business was coming soon. Noah had seen the same thing in the Midwest, where small stores came with a blaze of excitement and too often went out like a snuffed match within months. However, the doors to the bank on a corner beyond the hotel were opening and closing. Set on the opposite corner was a block building with wood decorating its high windows, and a door centered at the top of concrete steps. A sign identified it as the Lost River Public Library.

"Why do you call this town Lost River?" he asked Mollie, who'd been talking nonstop with his daughter and son. Why had she acted as if he wasn't there for the half-hour drive into town? She'd been sympathetic while he aired his frustration about today's meeting; then she'd acted as if he'd disappeared. She'd been delighted with his invitation to join him and his *kinder*, but a door might as well have slammed shut between them. Why?

Instead of asking that question, he went on, "When I heard the name *Lost River*, I wondered if this place would be a ghost town."

She looked at him for the first time since they'd left the school. Her face was placid, an unfamiliar expression, and he had to wonder what she was hiding. "When I asked my parents about the name, *Daed* shared the story our family was told when they migrated here from Missouri. To the east of us is the Great Sand Dunes National Park. Have you heard of it?"

"I saw signs for it when we came into the valley through the La Veta Pass, but I wasn't sure if it was real or a joke. Sand dunes in the mountains?"

"It's real. It… Oh, there's The Shivering Banana." She pointed to a storefront with a pink-and-green awning over the heavy wooden doors. The window had gold lettering with the shop's name and a picture of a banana with arms, legs and a face wearing a scarf and mittens on hands held out over what he guessed was supposed to be a pot of hot fudge bubbling over a campfire. "There's parking out back."

Noah steered the horse through a narrow alley between two buildings. When they emerged, he was pleased to see a hitching rail in the parking area. "I wasn't sure if they'd have a place to tie up."

"Plain folks have been living in this area for more than twenty years, so the merchants in Lost River want to make sure we feel welcome to *komm* and spend our money." Mollie stepped onto the asphalt and reached to lift out Sam, who was wiggling with excitement. "That's *gut* business."

"Without a question." He held up a single finger to warn Angela he needed to check something before he helped her. Pulling a rumpled piece of paper from his pocket, he scanned it. "Nope. The Shuddering Ban—"

"The *Shivering* Banana," Mollie amended while she got her bag.

"The Shivering Banana isn't on the list. Too bad. It would have been fun to create a barn quilt for them." He stuffed the paper into his pocket and swung Angela out of the wagon, earning more giggles from her.

Mollie led the way into a shop that looked like a candy factory. Examples of every sort of candy he knew—and plenty he'd never seen or heard of—were displayed on the walls above dispensers where customers could fill a bag with whatever they wanted. Angela and Sam pointed to everything, growing more excited until Mollie mentioned the ice cream was served at the front of the shop.

Noah forgot about candy once they were seated in a booth next to a large window. That table was covered in red gingham, but his attention was captured by the menu handed to him by a teenage waitress wearing a pink blouse, a frilly apron and a matching paper cap. Reading it, he wondered how he'd choose, let alone help Sam and Angela pick out something.

"Here's the kids' menu," Mollie said, closing his menu and turning it over. "Look at the clown sundae!"

"I want one!" Sam grinned. "With a bright green face."

"Do you like mint ice cream?" she asked.

He looked at Noah for an answer. "You don't like mint, son. Why not a blue face? That would be black raspberry, and you'd like that."

Sam nodded so hard he looked like one of the banana bobbleheads behind the ice-cream counter.

"What about you, Angela?" Mollie asked.

"I like strawberry ice cream."

"A *gut* choice. They've got the best strawberry ice cream here."

Satisfied, his daughter grinned.

Again, Noah was amazed how Mollie handled his *kinder*. She helped them, but let them make decisions, and she supported their choices, making them feel as if they'd achieved something. She assisted them placing their orders and then asked for a small hot-fudge sundae for herself.

He flinched when the waitress asked him what he wanted. He'd been listening to Mollie and hadn't chosen for himself.

Sam grinned and said, "My *daed* wants The Shivering Banana split!"

"Sir?" The waitress looked from him to his son.

"Why not?" he asked. "If I can't eat it all, I've got two assistants with bottomless pits for stomachs to help me." He winked at his kids, and they laughed.

While they waited for their ice cream and sipped the water that was welcome after the hot, dry drive, Angela and Sam became serious about coloring the place mats that had been set in front of them, along with small boxes of crayons. It gave him the chance to ask Mollie again about the origin of the name Lost River.

"*Daed* told me Lost River's name had to do with the Great Sand Dunes." She motioned out the window beside their table. "Look out there. You can see the San Juan Mountains past the roof of the visitors' center. They're the western edge of our valley. In the other direction are the Sangre de Cristo Mountains, which you passed through by taking the La Veta Pass. The winds blow from west to east. When dust particles are ripped off the western mountains, they blow across the valley." She ran her finger along the sill and smiled as she tipped it so he could see the smudge on it. "The dust that crosses the San Luis Valley is too heavy to rise over the eastern mountains. The particles fall to earth at the base of the mountains. They've amassed huge dunes of sand, the highest in the whole United States."

"Interesting, but what does that have to do with the town's name?" He rested his elbows on the table and propped his chin on his upturned palms. When Mollie had something to share with someone—to *teach* someone—her eyes came alive. She used her hands to emphasize her words and leaned forward, wanting the person she was talking to, whether a scholar or someone else, to be as excited about the information as she was. He found everything about her "teacher style" fascinating, and he couldn't have pulled his gaze away if he'd wanted to.

He didn't want to.

"It's simple. The snowmelt and rain off the slopes of the Sangre de Cristo Mountains goes underground before it flows far into the valley. It becomes the aquifer that makes farming possible. We don't get much rain or snow, though there are times when we get too much. So whoever named the town must have believed a river ran beneath here."

"Is there?"

"No." She grinned and shook her head at the same time. "Just the aquifer. A single river would mean the land could be cultivated only close to its shores."

"That worked for the ancient Egyptians."

"True, but have you seen a pyramid in town?"

When she laughed, he savored the sound. She had an uninhibited laugh. Perhaps it came from spending so much time with youngsters.

The waitress brought the *kinder*'s dishes along with Mollie's. When she returned, she brought what looked like a bowl big enough to mix several loads of bread. She set it in front of him and handed him a spoon with a knowing grin.

How did anyone expect him to finish what must be twenty scoops of ice cream, covered with toppings and whipped cream and crushed walnuts? Six split bananas marked milestones in the eating marathon ahead.

As the waitress walked away, he stared at the bowl in disbelief. "People eat all of this by themselves?"

"No," Mollie said with a laugh, "it's meant for four or five people. It says so right in the menu."

Not wanting to confess he'd been too distracted by her to

read the menu, he said, "I'm going to need help and prob-ably a stomach pump."

As he took his first taste, he knew Mollie had been right again. It was delicious, as *gut* as any in Wisconsin, which was renowned—as he'd been told while working on that barn-quilt-trail project—for its lush ice cream.

Noah hadn't made a dent in the delicious ice-cream mountain when Sam asked for a helping. Refilling his son's dish, he watched Sam take a quick bite, swallow it as if he hadn't eaten in days and jab his spoon back into it.

"Slow down, pardner," Noah drawled. "You'll get brain freeze."

"It's so *gut!*"

Mollie said, "There's lots more, so you don't have to rush. Enjoy each bite."

The little boy bobbed his head again, then took a slower bite.

How did she calm his son with a few words?

Again, Noah refrained from voicing the question in his head, but this time because Mollie asked him about what challenges he saw ahead for the barn-quilt project other than squabbling between the participants.

"The shape of barns here in the San Luis Valley is differ-ent from the Midwest," he said around bites of chocolate ice cream. "There, the gable ends are broader and taller. Here, several of the barns chosen for the barn-quilt trail have a more sloping profile. That's going to require quilts to be smaller in some places and taller and narrower for others."

She smiled. "So instead of having the quilts fit a single-size bed, you need to have quilts that fit twin beds along with those for doubles and queens and kings."

"As well as the custom beds for supertall folks or little kids."

"That will help you with different designs."

"True. I'll be looking to you and your quilt circle for advice and inspiration."

"It's going to be simpler to do that because you want nontraditional patterns for the barn quilts." She pulled Ruthanne's books out of her bag, then put them on the table beside him. "I meant to give these to you earlier. They're idea books my friend thought might inspire you."

He picked up the top one, set it on the table out of the range of the ice cream Sam had spilled and opened it to a random page. Bright colors and unexpected patterns exploded off the page. Then, as he examined them, he realized they were familiar. He'd seen the angles and colors in the quilt Mollie had been working on at her house when he and the *kinder* had first arrived.

When Mollie slid another open book on top of the one he'd been looking at, she said, "Here are images I thought you might be able to use. These pictures show the Old Spanish Trail monuments out on the road toward the San Juan Mountains." She smoothed the pages so he could see the wagon wheel carved into sandstone blocks. "Some are copies of ancient rock art in the area. I like the one with the parade of square-headed people around its base. Their bodies are shaped liked diamonds, and their arms are stretched out to one another."

He pointed to another carved chunk of sandstone. "This one is interesting, with a cloud higher along the rock and lightning flashing from it. I see a hand and what appears to be a flying serpent beneath it. Are those horses running along the bottom of the stone?"

"*Ja.* Are the images something you can use?"

"I can." He smiled at her. "You've got great artistic sensibilities, Mollie."

That pleasing flush warmed her face again, and it heightened when she looked past him as the front door opened. A group of men walked in. Most of them were close to his age. Was Mollie sweet on one of them? He felt as cold as if someone had dumped the massive bowl of ice cream over his head.

When Mollie stood and waved to the men, two of them walked toward the table. "It's time for you to meet Tyler and Kolton, Noah."

Tyler? Kolton? As she introduced her brothers to Noah and the *kinder*, Noah could see the similarities in the siblings' features around their eyes and their noses, but Mollie's face was a gentle heart shape, while her brothers had strong jaws that warned they were a force to be reckoned with in any discussion. Much like their sister.

Both men had sun-washed streaks in their light brown hair. Tyler reached out to shake his hand first. Kolton let his brother take the lead, but his handshake was firmer than his older brother's. While Tyler's blue eyes glittered with easy humor, Kolton's were watchful and cautious as he gave Noah a once-over.

"We tried to find you to talk after church," Kolton said, every inch the protective big brother. "We kept missing you."

"I'm sorry about that." He didn't offer any excuse, because he doubted the brothers were interested in hearing about how he'd been battling with himself. "Glad to meet you."

"Mollie doesn't talk about much other than you and your *kinder*." Kolton appraised him silently, then added, "I'm sure she's been a big help."

Tyler smiled at Angela and Sam, who were regarding him and his brother with candid curiosity. "I hear you're going to be stopping by the store some friends of mine own, Noah. They're on the list for a barn quilt."

Not sure which store it was, Noah nodded. "I've got a long list."

"So you're planning on staying in the valley for a while?" Kolton asked.

"As long as I've got commissions to paint."

"And then?"

Another blush flashed up Mollie's face. Did she think her brother was trying to ferret out what Noah's intentions were toward her? It was a legitimate concern since Noah was a stranger, and he and his *kinder* were monopolizing her time. Noah realized he didn't have anything to worry about when Kolton continued.

"We can use more volunteers at the fire department." He smiled, transforming his face. "When my class finished training last month, the chief's first instruction to us was to round up more volunteers. We're spread out here, and it can take too long to get to a fire in town. A vagrant spark and a high wind could turn the valley into an inferno. If a wildfire breaks out in the national forest…" He didn't need to finish.

An icy trickle ran down Noah's spine. Kolton didn't have to teach him about the dangers and consequences of fire. Noah was intimately aware of it. He kept his mouth shut before he spilled too much.

Before Kolton could say more, one of the men by the counter called him. He excused himself.

Tyler smiled. "Any chance you're a skier. Noah?"

"I'm afraid not. I grew up in hills, not mountains."

"That's too bad. How about a hiker?"

"Sometimes." He didn't add that the last time he'd gone on a hike had been before Angela was born.

"Maybe we'll head out sometime." He tapped his sister's nose. "See you tonight, *boppli*."

Mollie grimaced at him, making Sam and Angela laugh louder. Sitting at the table again, she pretended to pout as she grumbled, "I'm not a *boppli*."

That sent the *kinder* into renewed peals of laughter until she reminded them their ice cream was melting.

"Noah, forgive Kolton for being so pushy," Mollie said. "He's a new recruit, so he's doing everything he can to make the fire department a success. When God points us in a new direction, we have to learn to balance our joy with practicality." She glanced at where her brother was now ordering ice cream with his friends.

"I remember when I first learned I could draw and paint something besides walls. All I wanted was to explore what I could do." He chuckled. "That didn't last long. My kids needed my attention, and they weren't shy about letting me know." He picked up his spoon, then set it in the bowl. He'd eaten more than he planned. "Your brothers are right about one thing. I'm blessed to have your help. I wouldn't be as far along as I am on the project if you weren't there."

She blushed, this time because of his praise. As he'd expected, she changed the subject while she got the last bits of hot fudge out of her dish. The task let her focus on her bowl instead of looking in his direction.

"When will the first quilt be installed?" she asked.

"It's planned for next week. Would you like to watch us install it?"

When she didn't give him a quick answer, he wondered if she understood what he wasn't saying. She must know he needed to keep his *kinder* within sight. He couldn't take the chance of something catastrophic happening again.

"Ja," she said, smiling as if she'd replied without any

pause. "I'd like to go with you and the kids. It'll be fun to watch your hard work put on display."

Fun? He hoped he could remember how to have that because for the first time in five years, it sounded like a great idea.

Chapter Nine

The installation of the first barn quilt was delayed because of windy weather day after day. Under those conditions, it was too risky for Noah and the volunteers helping him to put the quilt in place. A gust could grab the big boards and turn them into painted wood kites, pulling someone off the scissor lift or tipping it over.

The time wasn't wasted. Noah went to work taping out the designs for his next three projects. One was a tumbling block quilt with its "fabric" decorated with plants and animals and birds found in the San Luis Valley. The second had a quartet of sheep, their feet pointed toward each other and the center, for the Detweilers' biggest barn. Around the outer edge were the star-shaped blossoms of the potato plants the family grew. He planned to paint them white with yellow seedlings at the center, as well as a few lilac-tinted blossoms, because the Detweilers also grew purple majesty potatoes, which were a lush violet inside.

The final one was Mollie's favorite. It had a simple field of potato blossoms in the main section, and the border was crenellated with mountain peaks that reached inward toward the middle of the quilt. It was set to be hung on the front of a huge Quonset hut that was used as a potato storage barn near the small town of Center, north of Lost River, on the Saguache County line.

When he'd decided he was going to do the quilts in the order he wanted to paint them and let the art-council members argue about which was hung next, Mollie could see he was relieved with regaining control over the project. She understood wanting to be in control. It allowed her schoolroom to run smoothly, and at the same time why she was distraught at having lost the memories for the weeks around the accident. It helped as she kept Angela and Sam entertained and quiet while their *daed* focused on his work. When she saw them looking at his paints, she brought watercolors for them to use on the large pieces of cardboard she got from *Doktor* Lynny.

The paints and cardboard weren't a *gut* match because everyone ended up soggy. Instead, she went into Lost River and purchased sketch paper, which absorbed the paint without becoming mush. The *kinder* showed off their creations when Noah stopped to join them for the midday meal. She left each afternoon around four to go home and prepare supper for *Mamm* and her brothers.

The pattern of her days wasn't broken until the following week when the weather got worse. The strongest windstorm yet swept across the valley, whistling at eaves and trying to steal everything that wasn't secured. It evolved into a sandstorm. The sky and the air turned a sickish yellow as blowing sand cut visibility to almost nothing. The sun was blotted out, and Mollie knew traveling through the blowing sand would be too dangerous for her and for her horse, Chester.

"I don't like that," Angela said, cuddling close to her. "The sky looks funny."

"It's not the sky. It's the air. It's filled with sand." She gave the little girl what she hoped was a cheerful smile.

Raising her voice over the roaring wind, she said, "You've never seen a sandstorm, ain't so?"

"No, and I don't like it."

"You'll be fine as long as you don't go outside."

Angela glanced at the door. "Our house is outside."

The little girl was right. Telling her to focus on her painting, Mollie went to where Noah was frowning at the fading light. His frown turned to concern when she explained what was happening.

"We don't have storms like this back east. How long do they last?"

"Usually less than twenty-four hours."

His puppy-dog-brown eyes caught her gaze. The concern in them warmed her from her heart out as he said, "You can't drive home in this."

"No. I'll stay here tonight if it hasn't dissipated. My family will know it wasn't safe to get home." A shiver went through her, though the air was warm. "I hope *Mamm* and Tyler and Kolton are safe at home."

"They know this valley as well as you do." He cleared his throat as he turned to peer out the window again. "Do you think we'll have to stay in the studio?"

"We don't have any food out here or much to drink. If we tie cleaning rags around our noses and mouths and cover the *kinder*'s faces, we can get to the bunkhouse. We'll want to keep our eyes closed as much as possible."

"That sounds like an invitation to landing on our noses."

She smiled. "It's not far. We'll aim ourselves in that direction and go."

"If it's still blowing when it's time to knock off, that's what we'll do." He put a hand on her shoulder. "*Danki*, Mollie. I don't know what we'd do without you."

She edged away from his touch before she found herself

stepping closer. Knowing she had to change the subject because his eyes glowed with warmth, she said, "I like your barn quilts, but they don't look like real quilts. They look like photos in books. Real quilts ripple from where we put stitches to hold the layers together. They get crumpled. They're not always finished."

"You think I should paint partially done quilts?" He looked astonished.

"No, but you could inject variety in them." She looked from one board to the next. "These are too perfect. Every quilter knows no quilt is perfect. Even if we redo stitches made in error, a faint line remains to reveal where the mistake was made. Sometimes we get deep into a pattern and realize we don't have enough fabric to repeat it the required number of times."

"So what do you do?"

"We improvise. There are ways to either hide mistakes or emphasize them so it looks to the world as if we intended the quilt to look like that right from the beginning. Don't you improvise with your paintings?"

"All the time." When he began to smile, a warmth spread through her. He was so serious that each grin was a unique gift. "I don't understand what you mean by making them less perfect. Other places where I've worked, they want the quilts to appear as if they're on the cover of a pattern book."

Mollie grabbed one of the quilts in the *kinder*'s play area. "Watch!" She hefted it high in the air and released it.

It floated in the air for a single heartbeat, then fell, draping itself on the *kinder* and the floor. She glanced over her shoulder and saw Noah's eyes narrowing as he appraised the colors and shadows created by the vagaries of the quilt's landing.

Angela crawled out from under the quilt. "Do it again, Mollie!"

"Later," she said, not wanting to be distracted from the point she was trying to prove.

"Let me think about this," Noah said.

When he picked up a pencil, Mollie knew he was already lost in his creative process. *Gut!* That meant he wouldn't regard her with such heat in his eyes, and she wouldn't want to melt in his arms. No, she longed to be enveloped in his arms, but she could force her mind to other things. Like how Angela was staring out the window at the storm. Sam, on the other hand, didn't seem the least distracted from painting horses in every possible color.

"It's going to be okay," Mollie assured the little girl, who was rocking one of her front teeth. Mollie hadn't noticed it was loose before, and she wanted to congratulate Angela, but the *kind* was too on edge from the storm. "Your *daed* and I have a plan to make sure we get to the bunkhouse and have a delicious supper."

Usually the talk of food soothed the little girl, but not today. She wrapped her arms around herself. "I don't like windy days."

"No? I do. I like to listen to the song the wind makes as it goes past the house. It's a soft lullaby."

The studio shook with a big gust as if to contradict her words.

Angela grasped on to her. "Will we blow away?"

"Can we?" Sam's smile widened. "I want to fly like an eagle. I could see everything."

"You couldn't today!" Angela walked away. When another buffet made the walls quiver, she sat and pulled her knees to her chest.

Mollie followed, kneeling beside her. "Angela, we'll be fine. Carlos and *Doktor* Lynny built these barns to withstand any storm. *Ja*, we've got to go outside to get to the bunkhouse, but once we're inside, we'll be as snug as a *boppli* in its *mamm*'s arms."

The wrong thing to say, she realized, when the little girl's face fell. "I don't have a *mamm*." Angela's lower lip trembled, and Mollie couldn't keep from wondering how much she remembered about Betty Jane. "You don't have a *daed*. That's sad."

"It is." She glanced at where Sam was mesmerized by his colorful horses. "We must be grateful God gave us others to love and whom we can love."

"Like my *daed* and your *mamm*."

"And our brothers."

Angela's face screwed up in an unmistakable expression of annoyance. "It's not easy to love a brother."

"I know." She laughed, thinking of Kolton's shoes in the middle of the living room. His coat and hat that never found pegs. Tyler walked a fine line between the life of a plain man and an *Englisch*er focused on skiing and other outdoors sports. She recognized he saw it as the way to help his family escape the burden of their debts, but she had to wonder whether he was thinking about his connection with God. Then she reminded herself of how distant her relationship was with her heavenly *Daed*. Not wanting to get mired in such uncomfortable thoughts, she said, "Angela, we must love them because they're our family."

"Even when my brother skips his bath after being out with Carlos and the horses?" Her button nose wrinkled. "He stinks!"

"*Ja,*" she replied, struggling to hold back her laugh. "Even when he stinks. My brothers used to stink something fierce, but that changed when they discovered having girls who aren't their sister think they're stinky was a bad thing."

"But they're grown-up men, ain't so?"

"*Ja.*"

"That means it's going to be forever until Sam stops smelling like a barn."

Mollie chuckled. "It'll take less time than you think, and when it happens, you'll see lots of changes in him. Remember, *gut* things *komm* to those who wait, but better things often *komm* to those who go out and work hard."

"Really?"

"Really," she answered, praying she was telling the truth.

Noah knew all about Mollie's upcoming meeting with other plain teachers in the valley. Not only had he read about it in *The Budget*, but she'd also mentioned it several times while they waited out the storm with his hosts, reassuring him he didn't need to worry about someone to watch his *kinder*. Since the sandstorm, he'd convinced himself her meeting was another week away, too lost in the never-ending clash among the arts commissioners to keep track of the passing days. The majority of the commissioners had decided to have the first barn quilt hung on the Fourth of July to be followed by more later in July and in August. It gave him almost another month to finish up the rest of the barn quilts he'd been working on, but the delay also meant the studio was growing more crowded with finished sections of quilts.

That was why he stared at Mollie, open-mouthed, when she poked her head into the studio and called, "Just stopped by to remind you I'll be gone today."

"You're not staying?" He put down the blue tape he was using to mark the pattern for another quilt, this one for a tack-and-saddle shop at the edge of town.

She entered, and he saw she was wearing her best. Her pale purple dress made her eyes a darker shade and brought out the dusty rose along her cheeks. She appeared nervous, but that didn't halt her from giving his daughter and son big hugs as she did every day when she arrived at the studio.

The *kinder* began to throw questions at her about what she had planned for the day, but she shook her head. "I can't stay. The teachers' meeting at my house begins in an hour." She looked toward him. "My friend Carrie Detweiler will be helping you today. She should be here soon."

"I can get along fine for one day," Noah replied while his kids groaned about not having fun that day with Mollie.

"I realize that, but she wants to help. You'll enjoy Carrie," she added to his *kinder*. "You know her from church."

"Why can't you stay?" Angela demanded, then stomped away with Sam close on her heels.

Noah shared their opinion. He didn't want a stranger in his studio. Even knowing that reaction was ridiculous didn't lessen it. After all, he hadn't known Mollie Lehman very long. Somehow, in a little more than a month, she'd become an integral part of his life and beloved by his *kinder*. He doubted lightning would strike twice, allowing Carrie to slip into their lives as easily, but they had to give the young woman a chance.

"Carrie is intrigued by the barn-quilt trail and the wooden quilts," Mollie said in a conciliatory tone. "She sees your work, Noah, as an extension of her own. She loves intricate and unique patterns." She laughed, but he sensed it was forced. "She loves to share the patterns she designs. Carrie is looking forward to spending the day with Angela and Sam." Worry tightened her mouth. "They'll be fine."

Will I? Noah was glad she wasn't able to hear his thoughts, but he couldn't ignore he was as disappointed as his *kinder* that Mollie wouldn't be with them today.

It's only one day, he told that nagging voice in his mind.

But you don't want to lose a single day with her, answered his heart.

Arguing with himself was worthless, but today he wouldn't hear Mollie's laughter mixed with Angela's and Sam's. That sound had inspired his work, urging him to use merrier colors and bolder patterns, as if joy could be captured on a signboard.

The rattle of buggy wheels announced Mollie's friend's arrival. His heart sank further, but he had a smile in place when she introduced him to her friend, who didn't look him in the eyes. There was an aura of shyness about the young blonde that made him question if she could handle his kids.

After Mollie bid them a *gut* day and told Noah she'd see him tomorrow, silence fell on the studio. The conversation that had been so easy with Mollie fell flat each time he tried to say something to her friend. He introduced his daughter and son to Carrie, then fled to his work.

For the first hour, everything went smoothly, but then Noah heard his *kinder*'s raised voices. He poked his head around the stall where their play area was. Angela had her hands on her hips while she glared at Carrie, and Sam was sobbing, his head buried in his arms, as if he'd been told every scoop of ice cream in the world had been consumed and there wasn't any left for him. Carrie was wringing her hands, trying to soothe the *kinder*, but they refused to listen to her.

He never did find out what had caused the outburst. Instead, he spent the next half hour calming Sam and Angela enough so he could leave them with Carrie. Fifteen minutes later, the uproar began again. Another half hour was spent regaining the peace, which lasted five minutes that time.

Recognizing he wasn't going to get any work done, he served a snack to the youngsters. Mollie had brought over two pans of brownies the previous day, and the *kinder* loved them almost as much as he did. Once they were settled, he offered Carrie a cup of *kaffi* from the pot on the table near his work area. She accepted and followed him toward the board where he'd been working. Now, quiet reigned.

"I don't know what's gotten into them," he said, seeing her distraught face.

"They miss Mollie." She stirred a packet of sugar into her *kaffi*. "She loves spending time with them."

And with me? asked that traitorous voice in his head. He pressed his lips together before the words escaped them.

"What do you think of Lost River?" Carrie asked when he didn't answer.

"I'm still finding my way around."

She smiled, and her eyes brightened. "It's not that hard. Almost everything is on a grid. I learned that after my family moved to the valley when I was a couple of years older than your daughter. Before that we lived in Somerset County."

"In Pennsylvania?"

"Ja." Her cheeks dimpled with her smile. "Are you familiar with the area?"

"I went there once with my youth group. We were curious about Amish who worship in a church building instead of each others' homes."

"Did you see a big difference?"

"Other than the building, no." He chuckled, pleased a conversation had gotten underway.

Looking across the stable, she said, *"Danki* for the *kaffi.* It looks as if Angela and Sam are done, too. Let's see if I can convince them to play."

Noah had his doubts, and they were borne out within minutes of Carrie returning to his *kinder.* As he picked up his paintbrush, he heard a furious shout from the other side of the building. With a sigh, he set down the brush, crossed the floor and spoke his *kinder*'s names. They ignored him.

"No!" Angela folded her arms over her chest and glowered at Carrie. "No, I won't. No, we won't." She stamped her foot.

Sam copied her motions, sticking his lower lip out so far Noah suspected he could balance a pencil on it.

"Please," Carrie begged, sounding overwhelmed.

"No!" his *kinder* said together.

"Angela!" he said, letting his voice crack like a buggy whip. "Samuel!"

They faced him, eyes wide. He couldn't remember the last time he'd spoken to them so sharply.

He held first his daughter's eyes and then his son's. "You may apologize to Carrie."

"*Daed*, she—"

"I'm not talking about what Carrie did. I'm talking about what you two have done. Carrie is a guest in the studio, and we treat guests with kindness."

The kids fired scowls at her.

Before Noah could say anything else, Carrie said, "It's clear this isn't going to work. I hate to leave you in the lurch, Noah, but it'll be better if I go."

"Not until they apologize."

He wasn't sure why he'd wasted his breath. His kids mumbled something that might have been an insincere apology, but when he was about to remonstrate with them, Carrie put her hand on his arm and shook her head. She was gone, leaving him no time to apologize himself.

What could he have said? That he was sorry for how his son and daughter had behaved. She knew that. That he regretted putting her through such a tough few hours. She knew that, too. That he understood why the *kinder* were dejected because Mollie hadn't been there because he'd felt the same.

He hoped she didn't know the last. That nobody did, but it was too late. His heart refused to be silent any longer. It wanted to be given to Mollie, who filled a void in his life he'd vowed by his wife's grave never to fill again.

Chapter Ten

Stifling a yawn, Mollie flipped the burgers in the pan. Salisbury steak had seemed like a simple choice for supper when she'd spent the whole day with local teachers. It was cooked on top of the stove, so she didn't have to light the oven and add to the oppressive heat in the kitchen. She glanced over her shoulder as the door opened and *Mamm* walked in.

Mamm gave her a single look, then asked, "What's wrong?"

"How do you do that?" Mollie let out a tired laugh. "How do you know what we're feeling before we say a single word?"

"A *mamm*'s intuition is a gift from God, and like all of His gifts, it needs to be used as often as possible." She hung her black bonnet on its peg. "You've got a long face for someone who's been looking forward to today for three months."

Mollie kept her eyes on the pan so she didn't have to meet her *mamm*'s. "I didn't enjoy it as much as I'd hoped."

Mamm opened the fridge, letting a puff of cooler air into the kitchen, and took out salad makings. She put them on the table and got a knife, then asked, "Why didn't you enjoy it?"

"I'm not sure. Last year, I'd been excited to participate in discussions. Today, it felt as if I'd heard it all before."

Mamm rinsed off the onions, lettuce and a handful of radishes before carrying them to the table. "From what you've told me, these conferences are aimed at newer teachers. You're well past that."

"Long past those first years." It wasn't easy to sound calm when *Mamm*'s words reminded her that most women spent a few years teaching before marrying. That wasn't the life God apparently had planned for her, and it shouldn't hurt, but it did.

More since she'd met Noah.

Silencing thoughts that would make her feel worse, she said, "Tyler is helping Kolton with evening chores. He got home before you did tonight."

"I stopped to deliver some molasses crinkle cookies to Howard Zehr."

Mollie's smile became more sincere. "You must have made his day."

"*Ja.* Howard can't bake the simplest item, though he cooks well enough for a widower."

"Sounds as if you've sampled his cooking."

A faint blush climbed *Mamm*'s cheeks that had been too pale in the months after *Daed*'s cancer diagnosis. "He sent tacos home with me the other night."

"The ones Kolton loved so much?"

"*Ja.*"

"Did you bring more?" asked her brother as he walked into the house. "You did tell Howard he's welcome to make those anytime again, ain't so?"

Mamm chuckled and shooed both of Mollie's brothers out of the kitchen. Water running in the bathroom moments later announced they were getting cleaned for supper.

As Mollie made mushroom gravy for the burgers, she didn't ask *Mamm* anything about Howard. *Mamm* had been visiting their neighbor more often in the past two months.

If *Mamm* wished to confide in her that she was walking out with Howard, Mollie would be glad to listen. But no questions. Not only was it impolite, but it would also open a door to let *Mamm* ask the questions Mollie had seen in her eyes—questions about Noah. That would have been unwise.

"Noah! Just the man I'd hoped to see," called a booming voice when Noah was on his way to his studio two mornings later. The air was too warm, and he wondered how long he'd be able to work before the heat became stifling.

His *kinder*, who acted as if nothing had been amiss yesterday, shouted and ran to give Carlos a hug as if he was an overgrown stuffed bear. They chattered like two exuberant chipmunks, asking when they could visit the herd of rescue horses again.

"You know *Doktor* Lynny is in charge of them," their host said with a big smile. "I hear she's bringing a pair of ponies home, and I'm sure she could use help once they're comfortable with us."

That brought excited laughter from the kids as they raced toward the studio.

"A pair of ponies?" asked Noah with an arched eyebrow.

"One pony can't carry two kids very far." He released his booming laugh. "It'll help Mollie when she needs to find them something to do to let off a little energy."

"You've been so generous. I can't let you take in two ponies because—"

His face grew somber. "I'm not doing it for you and the youngsters. Those ponies have been neglected, and Lynny has been itching to get her hands on them. Once they realize they're safe with us, they'll need to be exercised. Your kids will be the perfect solution. By the way, would you have time to add another quilt to the stack you've had ordered?"

"I can make time." He was grateful to his host and his veterinarian wife for making him and the *kinder* feel at home on their ranch. When was the last time he'd felt at home anywhere? Not since he'd left Lancaster County, that was for sure.

"Great! It's for the Lost River Animal Rescue. Once you've got your design ready, I'm going to ask Mollie and her circle of quilters to make an actual quilt which we can auction off to raise money for the shelter. However, the attention an auction brings is fleeting. A matching barn quilt to hang on the side of one of the animal-rescue buildings will keep people's minds on the need to find homes for the poor critters."

"That's an excellent idea."

"I try to have only excellent ideas." His deep laugh rumbled among the outbuildings. "Saves time in the long run."

"I'll have to try that myself."

"Let me know how it works out for you. Then I can figure out how it could work for me."

Noah chuckled along with Carlos. The man lived every day with zest.

"Do you have a pattern in mind?" Noah asked.

Carlos shrugged. "I don't know the first thing about designing quilts. Ask me about horses or cattle or sheep, and I can give you such a long litany of facts that you'll soon be dozing. Quilts? You'd be better off talking with Mollie about that."

"I'll do that."

"Then it's set." Carlos started to turn to head in a different direction, then paused. "Oh, I've been meaning to tell you. I hired a guy you should meet. He's come from Manitoba, where he's been working on a ranch for a couple of years. Name's Daryn Yutzy, and he's Amish like you.

Lived in Prince Edward Island before heading out to the Canadian plains."

Noah hid his surprise. "What's he going to do for you?"

"Wrangle horses and help Lynny train them so they can be adopted. He's been herding cattle, but when I talked to his former boss, I was told he's got a real feel for horses."

Noah felt his jaw drop. He hadn't ever heard of a plain cowboy.

As if Noah had spoken his thoughts aloud, Carlos said, "Don't look so surprised. There are a bunch of Amish cowboys in Wyoming and Montana who dress like the ordinary cowboys working the range. Some, from what Daryn tells me, wear clothes and a hat just like yours." He chuckled. "I don't know how they can keep a straw hat on when they're cutting out a calf, so I'm looking forward to a demonstration." With a wave, he walked toward the main house, leaving Noah to try to guess how many more surprises awaited him in the San Luis Valley.

Mollie balanced the sweating pitcher and four glasses on a tray. She cautioned Sam not to run in front of her, but he kept dancing around her in his excitement.

In fact, both *kinder* had been wound up that morning. At first, she'd thought it was because of the ponies Carlos had mentioned, but over and over, they told her how glad they were she was back.

To be honest, she was relieved to resume her work at Noah's studio after yesterday's disappointing conference. Was *Mamm* right? Had Mollie been too long in her job? She didn't want to wait tables as Carrie did, and she wasn't sure what skills she had other than working with *kinder*. The idea of becoming a nanny for another family was something she couldn't bear to think about because that would mean she wouldn't be working for Noah any longer.

"Mollie, can we go to the pond?" Angela asked, interrupting her thoughts. "It's so hot, and it'd be fun to go in the water."

"Can you swim?"

"I can," the little girl said, "but Sam can't."

"I can, too. Just not underwater." His nose scrunched. "I don't like to get my face wet."

Mollie focused on maneuvering around the youngsters. "Let's see what the day brings. See those clouds over the mountains? They mean we could get thunderstorms later."

"But not sandstorms." Angela shuddered as they reached the studio.

"If we get enough rain, the sand and dust will be plastered to the ground." She didn't add that thunderstorms and their winds sometimes stirred up the dust before the rains arrived.

Leading the way into the studio, Mollie gave her eyes a chance to adjust to the dimmer light. When she could see the table where she made *kaffi* each morning, she put the tray on it.

Noah was painting a deep navy blue center on a barn quilt. The finished ones sat, propped in pairs behind the boards he had yet to paint, in a stall. A single board was set apart, and she knew it was the smaller quilt he'd designed for the Lost River town hall, which was half of an old retail building.

She poured a glass and carried it to where he stood, appraising the board in front of him. When he turned with a smile, she thought her heart would burst right out of her chest and dance with joy.

"I thought you'd like lemonade," she said, proud of how serene her voice sounded.

"I'd love some lemonade. I didn't think it got so warm in Colorado in June."

She laughed. "It doesn't every year. In fact, some years we've had snowstorms during our end-of-the-year presentation at school."

"Everyone told me summers would be cool here."

"If you were on the peaks," she said as she filled two more glasses half-full and handed them to the *kinder*. "Here, we're more than seven thousand feet above sea level. A lot of the peaks we can see are thirteen thousand feet high or more. Tyler, who spends as much time as he can skiing in the higher elevations, says there's about five and a half degrees difference for every thousand feet you go."

"Your brother Tyler?"

"Ja."

"He spends a lot of time in the mountains?"

Going to where he stood, she clasped her sweating glass and leaned against the wall by the window, which gave her a view of the San Juan Mountains. The clouds had swallowed their peaks, and heat made the expanse between them and the ranch shimmer.

"Tyler loves to ski," she said, "and he's skilled at it. So skilled he was asked to join the ski patrol."

"There's a ski patrol in a valley that's as flat as a concrete sidewalk?"

She sighed. "That's the issue. He'd have to move into the mountains near one of the ski resorts. The closest one is nearly fifty miles away. His skiing buddies are *Englisch*, so they drive up there."

Her dismay at the thought of her brother going so far away must have sifted through her voice, because Noah asked, "Couldn't *you* hire a driver, if you wanted to visit him?"

"Of course, but I'm used to having Tyler around every

day. I'd miss him." She hoped her terse tone announced she was done discussing Tyler. Kolton, too, for that matter. She didn't want to own to her greatest fear. If Tyler left, would Kolton follow him? When they were younger, her two brothers had been inseparable. Did Kolton want to chase adventure, as Tyler did? Kolton had just completed his training as a volunteer firefighter. Would that be enough for him, or had he been bitten by the same bug as Tyler and would go to seek the next exciting thing?

So much had changed in the six years since her accident. Her long months of healing hadn't been done before *Daed* learned he had cancer. She'd tried to be strong for him and *Mamm* through unending chemo treatments and surgeries until he'd said enough, that he needed to surrender himself to God's will.

"You and your family are close." Noah finished his lemonade in a big gulp. "That's a blessing."

"I know, and I'm grateful for that. Since *Daed*'s death, family feels even more important."

He arched an eyebrow and went to refill his glass. "Like I said, you're blessed. You should be grateful. I would be."

"You *would* be? Do you think you're not blessed?"

He froze as he was reaching for the pitcher. Putting his glass on the tray, he faced her, "No."

Not caring what anyone thought, she took him by the arm and drew him out of his *kinder*'s earshot. "Is this about what happened when your wife died?"

"Ja." The word was ground out between his clenched teeth. "Our family was happy. *I* was happy. Then it was all taken away."

"I know." She locked her fingers together to keep from reaching out and touching him again. The air between was too charged for even the most casual contact. "Why are you blaming God for what happened?"

"Because He could have prevented it."

"You know it doesn't work like that. God's plan is for us to accept His grace and love into our lives. Everything else is up to us."

"It's not that simple."

"Why not?" She gestured toward where his *kinder* were building a house out of the boxes in which his supplies had been delivered. "Angela and Sam accept your love as a *wunderbaar* gift from you, their *daed*. As I did with mine." Tears blurred his face, but she blinked them back. "I know *Daed* loved me though he never told me so. Your *kinder* know you love them, though you may have never told them so."

"I have told them I love them in many different ways."

"God tells us He loves us in many different ways, too. Sometimes we have to listen within our hearts. Occasionally, His message is as loud as thunder."

"So you aren't angry about what happened that left you scarred?"

"How can I be angry when I don't remember what happened that night, Noah, or for a month afterward?"

"That's astonishing."

"I wouldn't describe it that way." She frowned. "I despise how hours of my life have been erased as if I were cleaning the blackboard. You're not wrong. I've been angry with God. I don't have to remember every detail of that night to know I could have died. I was found along the road. Alone and injured. I've heard speculation buggy racing was involved, but I don't know. What I do know is God didn't force me to be there that night. *I* made that decision. Every time I look in the mirror, I'm reminded how foolish I was."

"Do these hurt?" His fingers brushed the scars along her cheek.

Every answer she might have given him vanished at his touch. Her lips parted with a soft sigh as his skin caressed hers. A light burst into his dark eyes, a light that seared into her, opening corners of her heart that she had vowed to keep closed forever. His thumb coursed along her lower lip, and quivers shot through her. She wanted him to kiss her, to discover if the fire in his eyes was also on his lips. As his palm cupped her cheek, tilting her mouth toward his, she knew she'd been waiting for this moment her whole life.

A crash from the other side of the studio broke the enthrallment swirling around them. When a frightened, pain-filled cry came from the same direction, Mollie forced herself not to grab Noah and give him a swift kiss before responding to whatever had happened. She rushed to the *kinder*, and began digging out Sam from under a collapsed stack of boxes.

"He's okay," she said, looking at Noah, who was helping his daughter to her feet. "Just frightened."

"I'm not scared," boasted Sam as he wiped cardboard dust off his shirt. "That was a warning for Angela to watch out."

Mollie began laughing at the little boy's obvious attempt to save face, and Noah and his *kinder* joined in. The warmth that surrounded them was sweet, but it couldn't touch the cold at her center when she reminded herself that no matter how much she enjoyed being with this little family and no matter how much she longed for Noah to kiss her, this was temporary. They weren't her family, and after hearing Noah's powerful anger at the loss of his wife, she knew he wasn't ready to ask her to be a permanent part of it…even if she could have said, *Ja*.

Chapter Eleven

Nobody was around on the Marquezes's ranch when Mollie arrived. The pickups were gone, as was the wagon Noah drove. It was quiet. Almost too quiet, though the wind whispered through the trees edging the smaller paddock, where two ponies were grazing. One was white, and the other was black with white splashes across its coat.

Walking over, Mollie whistled. They raised their heads, then went back to grazing. She was shocked to see what looked like lacerations on the ponies' faces. Had someone cut them, or had they had a run-in with a fence? Either way, the cuts spoke of neglect.

"Angela and Sam are going to be thrilled to meet you," she said in the morning sunshine.

The white pony shook its mane, but the other didn't pause as it ate as heartily as her brothers had at breakfast when she'd made their favorite jalapeño bread.

After going to the buggy to get the loaves she'd brought to the ranch—one for the Fryes and the other for the Marquezes—she walked to the bunkhouse. She knocked on the door, though she guessed nobody was inside. A quick scan of the interior told her she was right. For a single moment, she was relieved. She wasn't sure how Noah would act today after they'd stood face-to-face yesterday, drawn together like steel to a magnet.

Mollie put the bread in the refrigerator and headed to the studio. Had Noah left her a note to let her know when he and the *kinder* would return? She didn't see one, so she gathered dirty clothes and towels before starting the first of what she guessed would be three loads of laundry. She swept and dusted and picked up toys to pass the time. After putting the first load of clothes into the dryer, she refilled the washer.

She took the broom, dustpan and a couple of rags in a bucket with her and headed to the studio. Maybe he'd left the note there, assuming she'd go there first.

The door to the studio was ajar. That startled her. Noah kept his studio closed when he wasn't there. He didn't want dirt or dust seeping in to mix with his paint. Who had left it open?

Dismay swept through her. Had he gone in such a hurry he'd left it unlatched? Too many thoughts of why he'd do that careened through her head. If Sam or Angela was hurt...

Shaking her head, she reminded herself it was foolish to look for trouble where there might not be any. Noah might have forgotten to close the door as he herded the youngsters outside. It wasn't always easy to keep Angela and Sam going in the same direction at the same time. Laughter bubbled through her as she thought of her own attempts.

As she stepped into the studio, her amusement vanished between one breath and the next. The space had been ransacked. Noah's supplies and the *kinder*'s toys were scattered and broken across the floor. Red paint was splashed everywhere.

She stared, unable to pull her eyes away. The paint flung across Noah's meticulous design of three painted ponies running with the wind didn't look accidental. Someone had wanted to destroy his work.

A shudder shook her almost to her core as the word *accident* echoed through her brain, sending sparks of pain from her head to her toes. She wasn't sure why, but the thought of an accident almost undid her. It was as if she was on a raft floating down a river swollen by a flash flood. Careening in every direction, out of control, going nowhere and everywhere at the same time. Was it a memory resurfacing and dragging her under at the same time?

Closing her eyes, she drew in a deep breath to steady her traitorous stomach, which wanted to embarrass her. She prayed when she reopened them, the damage to Noah's work would have vanished along with her queasiness.

The nausea dissipated, but nothing else changed.

The barn quilt Noah had been working on had been vandalized. With a soft cry, she turned toward the stall where he stored his completed barn quilts. More paint, red and yellow, had been thrown against the unused boards.

She grasped the one in the front. It was much heavier than she'd expected. Not caring that the paint was tacky enough to stick to her apron, she shoved the board aside so it was leaning against the other side of the stall.

"*Danki*, God," she breathed when she saw the barn quilt behind it was untouched. Peering between the boards, she discovered none of the completed sections had been damaged. Whoever had done this must have assumed that the only finished work was the one by the north-facing window.

That still left too many questions: Who had done this? And why?

Noah tried to hide his annoyance from his *kinder*. Carlos had told him Wendy Warner, the vice chairperson of the arts council, needed to see him as soon as possible to go over details for the first installation on Independence Day.

When Noah had gotten to the woman's realty office, she hadn't been there, and her assistant insisted there was no meeting with Noah on Wendy's calendar. Two hours wasted because of a misunderstanding.

He was glad his son and daughter weren't paying any attention to him. All they could talk about was a kitten waiting in the barn for them to play with when they got back.

When he pulled behind the main house on the ranch, his eyes widened at the sight of Mollie rushing toward the wagon, waving her hands over her head as if trying to land a plane.

"Noah! I've been looking for you!" she cried as he swung down from the wagon.

He was glad he could turn to get his kids out so she didn't see his smile. It had to have revealed his delight with her bold words. Making sure the smile was gone by the time he faced her, he didn't have a chance to reply.

Angela, who'd run into the barn as soon as her feet hit the ground, said from behind Mollie, "Look what we've got. *Doktor* Lynny brought her to us last night." Angela held up the black kitten with patches of gold on her nose. It was tiny, no more than six weeks old. "Her name is Mariposa. That means butterfly, you know."

As his daughter cooed to the kitten, Noah said, "*Doktor* Lynny was feeling bad the kids can't play with the ponies yet, so she decided to lend them another animal to take care of."

"Noah—"

"I know. I should have spoken to you about the kitten before I agreed. Angela has said she'll take care of it, but I know how those promises can be broken if she gets distracted by something else."

"Noah—"

"Let me reassure you, Mollie. If the kids don't take care of the kitten, I will. You won't have to—"

She grasped his forearms, startling him. She'd been careful to stay away from him since yesterday afternoon, after he'd foolishly drawn her to him. No, not foolishly. He couldn't remember wanting anything more than her kiss, but she was a *maedel*, and a kiss to her would mean he had intentions of asking her to be his wife.

He wouldn't do that. He wouldn't endanger her by being a careless husband as he had with Betty Jane.

"Don't go in the studio," she said, her voice low, intense, almost desperate.

"Why?"

She faltered, then said, "Don't take the *kinder* in there. Tell them to play with their kitten out here."

"You know I like to keep them within sight."

"Just this once, Noah. Please keep them out until you see what's inside."

He saw how agitated she was. She was struggling to restrain her feelings so the kids didn't notice. What was she trying to hide from them?

If Sam and Angela were surprised by him telling them to play outside with the kitten, they were too busy petting Mariposa to show it. He almost changed his mind and told them to *komm* inside, but Mollie's tug on his arm stayed his words.

She didn't speak, either, as she led the way into his studio. He didn't need to wait for her to clear the door before he saw the malicious destruction that had been wrought on his studio. Nothing was where it should be. Paint cans had been opened, and their contents had been splattered everywhere.

He couldn't halt the groan that burst past his lips when he saw paint spread across the barn quilt he'd almost finished for the tack shop. Hours of hard work had been destroyed, and he would have to try to fix it before the installation date in the last week of July.

"It's horrible," Mollie whispered.

"It's fixable." He was glad to push aside his fury long enough to offer her comfort. Himself, too. Saying it was repairable made him believe it would be. "Nobody was hurt."

"The other barn quilts are okay. Whoever did this must not have realized you kept the completed ones behind the unused boards in the stall." Her voice broke as she asked, "Who would do something like this?"

"The person who told Carlos I was wanted at a meeting in Lost River so urgently I needed to bring the *kinder* with me."

A single tear ran down each cheek as she breathed, "*Danki*, God, for you not being here when this happened."

Noah wasn't feeling grateful to God or anyone else. He crossed the open space, then kneeled to inspect the damage. He had two options. One was trying to remove the top layer of paint with paint thinner. The other was to repaint over the damaged areas. Either option would require hours of extra work.

Standing, he explained to Mollie why he and his kids had been away. She listened without comment until he was finished. She didn't speak straightaway. The sounds of excited chatter came from where the kitten was entertaining Sam and Angela.

"You don't suspect Carlos of having anything to do with this?" she asked at last.

"No!" His own vehemence startled him. "Carlos and *Doktor* Lynny have offered nothing but kindness to us. They're one-hundred-percent behind the barn-quilt-trail project."

"What about Wendy, the arts commissioner?"

"She'd be pretty stupid not to give herself an alibi. If she'd sent me the note to get me out of here, wouldn't she have made sure she was in her office when I got there?"

"Then who…?"

"There are some among us who see my work as inappropriate for a plain man." Bitterness burned like acid in his mouth.

"I don't know anyone in Lost River who would think that." She looked at the ruined barn quilt, then at him. "The people in our community have welcomed you and your *kinder.*"

"People don't always say everything in their minds." He bent to pick up a broken brush. "Or in their hearts."

As he straightened, he saw comprehension burst through her like sunlight in the wake of a thunderstorm. "Who denounced your work before?"

"There was a family in Wisconsin who believed I was doing everything for my self-glory instead of celebrating a community." His lips twisted in a taut sneer. "They weren't in the district where I was working, but they—"

"No!" She hurried on when he regarded her with shock at her interrupting him again. "I can tell you didn't really care about that family's opinion, and I can also tell there has been at least one person whose opinion you do care about who has denounced your work." Her eyes grew round. "Not your wife?"

"No!" He worked to control his anger. "Sorry, Mollie. I shouldn't have shouted at you."

"It's okay. We're on edge."

He longed to pull her close, wrap his arms around her, find her lips and close the two of them off from the rest of the world. He mustn't, so he said, "I started painting after Betty Jane's death. If I'd begun before, I'm sure she would have supported me." He swallowed roughly. "That is, I assume she would have, though her parents don't."

"How do you know? Did they confront you?"

"No. I haven't spoken to them since I left Pennsylvania. But words have wings, and they reach far beyond the place and the time when they were uttered. What I've heard I'm glad the *kinder* haven't."

"Nonsense!"

He stared at her as if she'd sprouted wings herself. "What do you mean?"

"What I mean is you can't condemn someone for saying words you haven't heard yourself. How many times were those words repeated from the time they left your in-laws' lips until they reached your ears? Have you forgotten the game *kinder* play where they whisper into each other's ears what they think another *kind* has whispered in theirs? By the time the words go around a circle of a half-dozen youngsters, the original ones have been blurred or obliterated. Is the gossip flowing along the Amish grapevine any different?"

"No." His long-held anger at Japheth and Jane Klingler eased as it hadn't in the two years since he'd heard the rumor.

"*Mamm* has a favorite verse from Colossians 4:6. 'Let your speech be always with grace, seasoned with salt, that ye may know how ye ought to answer every man.'"

"In other words, don't believe everything you hear."

"But say what you mean, and what I mean to say right now is we need to contact Jerek."

"The bishop?"

"He'll want to know about this."

Noah's answer was interrupted yet again. Not by Mollie this time, but by two loud *kinder*, who rushed into the studio, then stopped as if striking an invisible wall.

"Wow!" Sam turned around to take in the devastation.

"Wow!" repeated his sister.

The kitten mewed, and Angela set her on the floor. Mariposa began to nose around, curious about everything.

"What happened?" Sam asked.

"We're trying to figure it out," Noah said, though he wanted to keep the youngsters from realizing the damage was intentional.

Both kids tiptoed around the scattered items on the floor and edged closer to the barn quilt. Sam laughed.

Noah saw his own shock reflected back to him from Mollie's face, then she asked, "What's funny, Sam?"

"This is," the little boy said, bending over to look at the barn quilt from another angle. "Look, *Daed*! Here's a puppy and a goat standing by a campfire." He giggled. "They look like they're sniffing the fire."

Angela stepped closer to her brother and contorted herself to appraise the plank as well. "No, it's not a goat, Sam. It's a cow. See? There's her udder."

"No, that's part of the fire." He gestured to a spot where the bright crimson paint was splattered over the hooves of the ponies. "Cows don't have red udders."

"They do when *Daed* paints them." She smiled at him. "Isn't that right, *Daed*?"

Noah blinked, uncertain how to reply. The last thing he'd expected was to hear his *kinder* laughing at the destruction of the barn quilt. Then he realized he should be grateful for their innocence that allowed them to see the damaging paint as a possible new pattern he'd created.

God, danki *for their sweet eyes and loving hearts*, he sent up before he had a chance to think. What once had been a common reaction was a *wunderbaar* revelation. Odd that he'd have this brief, blessed connection in the midst of the havoc meant to tear him apart.

"Can you see the cow, Mollie?" asked Angela as she wiggled her loose tooth with one finger.

Mollie drew his daughter's hand away from her mouth. "You need a *gut* imagination to see it."

"*Ja*, you do," insisted Angela. "You told us the story 'bout the turtle who talked to the birds yesterday. When Sam asked to go and visit the turtle, you said it was your maj-nation."

"I did, ain't so?" Mollie's smile brought answering grins from his *kinder*. "I like telling stories, but I'm not as *gut* as you are at picking out animals from the paint. That's your imagination, and it's special."

Again, Noah was astonished. He'd never heard a plain *kind* being lauded for being special. It had been better, in his school, to fit in with the other scholars. He'd been taught everyone had gifts from God, but they weren't anything to boast about. That was why he'd hidden his joy in painting until an *Englisch* guy on the construction crew where he'd been working discovered one of his pictures and had pestered Noah until he admitted it was his work. As soon as he said that, the *Englischer* had shared that with everyone, who lauded Noah on how talented he was. The construction team's boss, later that day, had asked Noah to paint a mural the homeowner had spoken about and nobody had the skills to do. That small push had nudged Noah onto the path he now walked.

Again, he prayed: *God,* danki *for Your presence at the turning points of our lives. Help me to see that this is one as well.*

Mollie startled him when she said, "Amen."

"Did I say what I was thinking aloud?" he asked after she'd sent the youngsters to start collecting the toys.

"You didn't need to. My heart heard your pain and your gratitude, because it's mine, too."

He held out his hand, and she put her own on it. Neither of them spoke. There wasn't any need. She must have known, as he did, that this moment was fleeting, but it was one he would treasure the rest of his life.

Jerek Stahl, the bishop of the Lost River districts, wasn't an impressive-looking man. He was of slight build, not much taller than Mollie. His dark beard appeared flimsy, but was wispy and ragged at the bottom. He had the ability to chat with anyone. He spoke with a slight lisp and often paused to think before replying, giving strangers the impression he wasn't paying attention. One glimpse of his dark brown eyes erased any concerns about his ability to serve as the bishop for the two Lost River districts, the other as far north of the town as Mollie's district was south. His expressions were stern while at the same time invited everyone to open their hearts and let him help them.

That was why, when Mollie stood in Noah's studio and waited for the bishop to speak, she wasn't disconcerted by Jerek's silence. The bishop had greeted the *kinder* with an easy smile as he arrived. He nodded in her direction and in Noah's before he strode to the ruined barn quilt. He'd done that more than five minutes before, and silence had settled in the barn. Faint shouts from where Angela and Sam were playing with the kitten filtered into the studio.

Folding his hands behind his back, Jerek looked at them. "You're Noah Frye, ain't so?"

"*Ja.*"

"This is your work?"

She could tell that Noah wasn't sure how the bishop would react to a plain man doing such huge art, but he said, *"Ja."*

"Has this happened to you before?"

"No, never."

"I don't mean here in Lost River. I mean anywhere."

"My answer would be the same. I've never had any damage done to my barn quilts while I'm painting them. Once in Indiana, half of a quilt fell while it was being hung, and that portion was ruined. I was able to recreate it from my drawings. The big difference is that damage wasn't malicious."

Again, Jerek was silent. Mollie wanted to reassure Noah that the bishop wasn't judging him. Instead, Jerek was considering everything he'd been told before his next question.

"You think *this* was a malicious act, Noah?" the bishop asked almost a full minute later.

"I don't know how it couldn't be."

The bishop turned his steady gaze on her. "What about you, Mollie? Do you believe this was done on purpose?"

"Ja," she said without hesitation. "Noah is careful with his supplies, and he never leaves the door open when he's not here. I found it unfastened when I came out here. When I walked in, I saw the damage done to his painting."

"So do either of you have any suspects in mind? The police will want to know."

Mollie flinched. Matters among the plain people were handled without getting the authorities involved. Jerek must think that this was something that reached beyond the *Leit* to *Englischers*. As she did.

Yet to hear the bishop speak of that drove a deep chill through her. This time, a single barn quilt had been damaged. Next time...

She didn't want to think of that.

Chapter Twelve

Mollie checked the picnic cooler she'd prepared for the Fourth of July. It contained food, books and projects to entertain Noah's *kinder*. She guessed that because they'd witnessed their *daed* hang a barn quilt before, Angela and Sam would grow quickly bored.

As it seemed the police had become with the investigation into the person who'd thrown paint on Noah's barn quilt almost two weeks ago. An officer had come to the ranch to interview her and Noah, as well as Carlos and *Doktor* Lynny and their employees. Nobody had seen anything to help identify the perpetrator. *Doktor* Lynny had been handling an emergency visit to the east in Alamosa, and Carlos had been with friends in town. None of the ranch hands had been close enough to the studio to notice anything unusual. Two other police officers had spent time examining the studio. They'd told Noah as soon as they had something to share, he'd be the first one to know.

Instead of being discouraged by the damage, Noah had been galvanized. He'd spent hours on his knees dabbing thinner on the red paint and removing it. Paint underneath had come away, too, but he'd assured Mollie and his hosts he could fix the spots. She was glad he shared that information with the Marquezes, because they couldn't conceal how bad they felt about the whole incident occurring on their ranch.

"Sorry we've taken so long," said Noah as he and the *kinder* emerged from the bunkhouse. For once, the kitten wasn't in Angela's arms.

Mollie wondered how Noah had convinced his daughter to leave Mariposa behind, but didn't ask while she helped the youngsters into the wagon. There was the picnic basket and the old quilt she'd brought for them to sit on while they watched their *daed* hang the inaugural barn quilt.

She was about to climb on the seat when Noah asked, "Can I show you something before we leave?"

"We'll be late if we don't get going."

He laughed. "They're not going to start without us."

"Without you."

"One and the same." When he held out his hand to her, it felt natural to put her fingers on his palm. Ripples of something delicious rose up her arm from where her skin brushed his on every step they took. He acted unaware of the incredible sensations because he continued talking as if he held her hand every day. "I've been working on something new."

"Another barn quilt?"

"*Ja* and no." He led her into the studio. "Wait here." He walked past her to a large board that had a paint-splattered sheet draped over it.

She'd noticed it there before, but hadn't paid much attention because she'd been concentrating on the repairs he'd been doing to the painted ponies barn quilt. That one still had a few areas left to fix.

"Ta-da!" he announced as he pulled the cloth away.

She stared at a barn quilt she hadn't seen before. Unlike the others, it wasn't static, balanced with colors and design. Instead, Noah had put what appeared to be depth where each "stitch" had been taken. The quilt's "fabric" bunched at the left side near the bottom, and she could see where a thread and needle had been painted as if they'd been inserted into actual material, waiting for the quilter to finish a quilted leaf.

Drawn by the barn quilt's extraordinary realism, she reached out, but yanked her fingers back.

"It's okay. It's dry," he said.

"It looks real." She couldn't pull her gaze from the barn quilt to look at Noah's smile. He must have been smiling. She could hear it in his voice. "This is nothing like the others you've done."

"You challenged me to do something different, something a quilter could recognize as a project in process, so I tried."

"You succeeded." She clapped her hands in delight. "Noah, everyone is going to be so excited about this. It's unique."

"I hope not. I hope I can devise others as interesting as this one." He put his hands on her shoulders and turned to her face him. "*Danki*, Mollie, for being my inspiration."

"We helped," Sam said, bouncing through the door.

"By being *gut*," Angela added. "As you told us to, Mollie."

"See how you inspired all of us?" Noah's fingers curved to cup Mollie's elbows. His smile became so intimate her toes urged to her to rise to meet his lips. The thought warned her how her longing for his kiss was growing. She breathed in tempo with him, and she wondered if his heart was beating as swiftly as hers.

"Did you see Mariposa?" asked Sam as he grasped her hand.

Stepping away from Noah was one of the toughest things

she'd ever had to do. She glanced around. The kitten had been banished from the studio last week after trying to drink paint-tainted water.

"No," the little boy said. "Not in the studio. There!" He pointed to the barn quilt. "At the bottom."

Mollie looked at what she'd dismissed as an unfinished portion of the image. Looking closer, she realized the darkness was the kitten's black fur. Noah had painted the kitten's golden nose against one side of the quilt, and her two bright eyes with an annoyed expression. A single paw was stretched toward the viewer, as if the kitten was wiggling from under a heavy quilt.

"I had no idea you could paint like this, Noah!" she said with another gasp. "It looks as if Mariposa is about to step out of the board."

"Carlos and *Doktor* Lynny asked me to do a barn quilt for the local animal shelter. They thought it would lead to more abandoned animals being adopted."

"What a *wunderbaar* idea!"

He grinned. "It didn't take any convincing to make me realize, too, that it was. I created this trompe l'oeil barn quilt with a kitten to remind people of the animals needing to find homes."

"Trompe…what?"

"Trompe l'oeil is a French term. It means to deceive someone's eye."

She laughed. "It'd fool mine. If I didn't know better, I'd say that was really Mariposa."

"I held her," Angela said, "while *Daed* drew her into the picture."

"You did a *gut* job." She gave each *kind* a hug. Not looking at Noah because she didn't want him to see how much she wished she could embrace him, too, she said, "We need to go, or we'll be late and won't get a *gut* seat to watch your *daed* hang the first barn quilt in Lost River."

The kids ran out of the studio while Noah put the sheet over his newest creation. An icy frisson sliced down Mollie's back as she realized why he did that before double-checking the door was locked. Only then did he join them at the wagon. He didn't want to give anyone the opportunity to do more damage to his barn quilts.

"I should stay here," she said after they'd climbed onto the front seat of the wagon. "The Marquezes will be there, too. Everyone knows that." She chose her words with care, not wanting to frighten the youngsters.

"Carlos and I discussed that." He pointed to a tall, young man who was sitting on the bunkhouse's front porch, where he'd have a *gut* view of the studio. His blond hair caught the sunshine from beneath his straw hat. "That's Daryn Yutzy, Carlos's newest hire. He'll be keeping an eye on the studio. Just in case."

"I'm so glad to hear that."

"Me, too." He handed her the reins and bent to check the toolbox by his feet. Pulling out a well-used hammer, he examined the handle. "This is the day when everything I've worked on comes together. The day when the barn quilt stops being mine and will now belong to everyone."

"It must be sweet and bittersweet. Like when a *kind* first goes to school and begins to build a family of friends to add to his or her birth family."

"I've been warned there may be a crowd today. Carlos mentioned Mark Tremble would be there. Do you know who he is?"

"He's a photographer and a reporter for *The Lost River Review*, the local newspaper. I'm surprised he hasn't already asked to interview you or take photos of your studio and works-in-progress."

He dropped his hammer and flinched, though it'd missed his toe.

"If they want to take pictures," she said, "and you're uncomfortable with that, they'll understand. Our *Englisch* neighbors try to understand our ways and accept them as we try to understand and accept theirs." She took her gaze from the road as she faced him. "Or is it that you don't want your name or face published anywhere? Not in *The Budget*. Not in *The Lost River Review*."

"I prefer to shun any publicity."

"Then you're in the wrong occupation. The installation of these barn quilts is all anyone in town was talking about yesterday."

"I should let someone else hang the quilt."

"Noah, people are going to want to meet the artist. You know that. How did you avoid this in other places?"

He put the hammer into the box and latched it shut. "I told them plain folks don't want their faces in photographs or their names in *Englisch* newspapers."

"Then do the same here. Mark respects our ways, and our bishop has spent time with him to explain how *hochmut* is something we deplore. None of us want to be set above the others in a prideful manner."

"I hope you're right," he said.

She hoped she was, too.

The crowd stood in the center of Main Street anywhere there was a view of the town barn. There were more people than Mollie had expected. Had every person in the San Luis Valley joined in to watch the first barn quilt be put in place? After Noah was whisked away by the arts commissioners, who were airing their opinions on every aspect of the installation, she looked around to find a place where the *kinder* would have a *gut* view of the whole event.

She was shocked when Iris Zavala, the mayor of Lost River, approached and asked if she was Mollie Lehman. When she nodded, the mayor, who wasn't much older than Mollie, asked her and the *kinder* to follow her.

"We've got a place for you," the dark-haired mayor said with a beaming smile as she took the quilt Mollie had brought. "We want to make sure the kids get to see their father."

"*Dan*— Thank you." Mollie settled the picnic basket over her arm, took each *kind* by the hand and followed the mayor, who had a remarkable skill of wending her way through the press of spectators without annoying anyone.

"We're excited about this barn-quilt raising," the mayor said.

"Barn-*quilt* raising?" Mollie chuckled. "I like that."

Everybody had a broad smile for Angela and Sam, who, after a moment of uncertainty, grinned back. The happy, holiday mood continued as they went to the front of the gathering, where a roped-off space had been saved for them. It was bigger than she and the youngsters needed.

Mayor Zavala told her to invite whomever she wished to join them. After pulling the rope off the stakes that had marked the spot, the mayor wound it around her arm. She vanished into the crowd after telling them to enjoy their day.

As Mollie was getting the *kinder* settled on the quilt and setting out toys to keep them entertained, she saw no sign of Noah or anyone else involved in the installation. She guessed they were in the barn, checking the equipment and the barn quilt's four pieces.

"Mollie!" At the call of her name, she saw her friends Ruthanne and Carrie. They waved to her. Albert, Ruthanne's fiancé, was with them, but when the women came forward to join Mollie and the *kinder*, he slipped into the crowd without a greeting. Not that it was difficult for him to disappear. Albert had mousy brown hair and a face too narrow for his patrician nose. Of average height, he never stood out in any crowd. He appeared to be the most self-effacing man in Lost River, but he had an adventurous streak that rivaled her brothers'. No skiing or fighting fires for Albert. He liked speed. He never pushed a horse beyond what it was capable of, but there were rumors he'd been involved in plenty of buggy drag races. He took too much pride in those triumphs for a plain man…at least in Mollie's opinion.

Mollie greeted her friends, but wondered what Albert's problem was. He hadn't said anything to her in months. Or had it been longer? She wasn't going to let Albert's odd behavior ruin this special day. She invited Ruthanne and Carrie to sit with them.

"Ruthanne, will you keep an eye on the kids?" Carrie asked, "We'll go and—"

"I must stay with Angela and Sam," Mollie said.

"Ruthanne will watch them while we get ice cream for everyone, ain't so?"

Mollie didn't have time to protest before Carrie wrapped her arm around hers and tugged her toward a food truck on the corner. Mollie relaxed when she discovered she could keep an eye on the youngsters from the long line waiting to order.

Carrie became serious as soon as they were out of Ruthanne's earshot. Such an expression was rare on the younger woman's face. "Can I be blunt, Mollie?"

"*Ja.* Always."

"You need to stop matchmaking."

"Me? Matchmaking?" Mollie shook her head. "I don't do that."

"*Ja*, you do. You tried to match me with Noah Frye."

"What?" The word came out in a gasp.

"When you asked me to take care of his kids."

Mollie flinched. Had Carrie read her thoughts at the quilting circle? Mollie had thought about the possibility of a match for her friend and Noah, but hadn't spoken about it. "If you remember, I didn't ask you. Well, I did, but because you offered to watch Angela and Sam."

"True, but you can't deny you were excited about the idea of me spending time with Noah."

"Of course, I was. I had my teachers' conference, and I knew I could depend on you."

"Don't get me wrong," Carrie said as she motioned for Mollie to get in line ahead of her. "Noah is a nice guy, but he's almost ten years older than I am. I want to spend time with someone closer to my age. If you want to make a match for someone, Mollie, you should be thinking about making one for yourself."

Cold seeped deep into her center at the thought of telling a man she'd never be able to carry a *boppli* to term. A man wanted a wife who could give him a family.

She tried to listen when Carrie kept talking, relating how Angela and Sam had made it clear they didn't want her around, that they wanted Mollie instead. That should have made Mollie feel better. It didn't. She couldn't let Noah's *kinder* become too dependent on her, because someday Noah might decide to remarry, and she didn't want to cause problems for his future wife.

Who wouldn't be Mollie Lehman.

When Mollie returned to the kids, Ruthanne immediately turned the subject to her wedding. Carrie rolled her eyes, and Mollie guessed the younger woman had already been listening to Ruthanne's obsessing about the cake Mollie's *mamm* had agreed to bake.

"Can I help frost the cake?" Angela asked when Ruthanne mentioned having light blue frosting.

"I'll lick the bowl!" Sam insisted from where he was stacking blocks to make a barn for two plastic horses with the same names as the ponies *Doktor* Lynny was fostering.

"*Mamm* will make that decision." Mollie didn't want to commit her *mamm* to having the *kinder*'s help. "I'll let *Mamm* know what color frosting you want, Ruthanne. Does Albert have any preferences?"

"He said it's up to me." Ruthanne smiled as if she'd received the greatest gift, though Mollie had a sneaking suspicion Albert didn't want to go over and over every detail. "I'd like you, Mollie, to talk to him about his input on who will be sitting with whom for the evening meal."

"I don't know if I can do that."

"Why?"

"Albert's been avoiding me."

Ruthanne raised her eyebrows in shock. "Are you sure of that?"

"*Ja.*"

"Why is he avoiding you?"

Mollie hesitated, then said, "I don't have the slightest idea, but when you came over, he headed in the opposite direction."

"He's been bothered since those boys near Alamosa crashed their buggies while drag racing. Not bothered. Angry."

The mention of buggy racing struck Mollie like a slap across the face. Had someone been hurt, as she'd been? Assuming she'd been in a buggy racing along the straight valley roads. Before that question could burst out of her, Mollie asked, "How's your sister doing with her new daughter?"

"According to *Mamm*, she's doing well."

"I'm glad to hear that. I—"

An eager rumble came from the crowd, and Mollie glanced up to see people emerging from the town barn. When Sam shouted, *"Daed!"* she smiled at her friends and turned to watch the proceedings.

She prayed it would go well for Noah, and that it was the first of many successful—and safe—barn-quilt raisings.

"Steady there," said the project foreman as Noah stepped onto the yellow scissor lift's platform almost an hour later. He'd begun to wonder if he'd have a chance to hang the barn quilt before sunset *three days from now* because every official in town and beyond had made a speech. Most had kept their comments to a minimum, but the arts-council chairman, Brant Hunter, had droned on for fifteen minutes. Brant took complete credit for every aspect of the project, not bothering to thank his fellow council members or Noah.

The gate on the scissor lift closed behind Noah and the foreman when the chairman stepped aside to tepid applause. Locked into place, the gate would keep them from falling. Noah turned to where the pieces of the barn quilt had been strapped to the rails. He'd been shown how to release them and, just as important, how to keep them from tumbling out. Though he'd used similar equipment in the past, he listened closely to the safety information. One wrong move could be deadly for those in the air and those on the ground.

Shrugging on the harness, he nodded to the project foreman, a guy everyone called Boomer. Noah wasn't sure why. The man wasn't loud in any way.

"Here we go," Boomer said as he switched on the hydraulics that raised and lowered the lift.

It grumbled beneath Noah's feet. Hooking himself to the metal railing, as he'd been instructed, Noah held his breath as Boomer worked the controls while they rose in the air. He sensed the eyes aimed at them as they climbed along the building. A glance over his shoulder made him smile. Angela and Sam were with Mollie right where he could see them.

"Your kids?" asked Boomer.

"Ja."

"Nice-looking wife you've got."

"She's not my wife. She watches my son and daughter while I work. My wife died five years ago."

Boomer whistled. "Sorry about your wife, man, but I've got to say that gal is pretty."

"She is," he said, but under his breath, so the sound vanished beneath the creaking of the unfolding lift.

Hanging the barn quilt went smoothly. The frame that had been attached to the building was level, and the lift reached high enough so he didn't have to stand on tiptoe and strain to reach the top. He was able to secure the sections with ease, using his hand tools and the power ones loaned to him by the public works crew. Boomer handed him a level for a final check. The project manager turned to the crowd and gave a thumbs-up as Noah lowered the tool.

A cacophony of cheers and hoots and car horns broke out as the lift lowered toward the ground. Several people rushed forward, tossing questions in Noah's direction. They were motioned aside by police officers, who stepped between them and the lift.

"C'mon," complained one older man whose graying hair was thin. "Give us a chance to interview him."

The officer in charge said, "You'll have your chance to talk to him, Mark, when it's safe. You should know better."

"I need to talk to him before those kids post their phone videos. If…"

Noah didn't listen to anymore as he realized the man must be Mark Tremble, the reporter. Realizing the threat to his anonymity wasn't just from the local newspaper, but also from social media, he hastily unhooked himself from the safety harness. His in-laws wouldn't be on those platforms, but he wasn't naive. Amish teens were as fascinated with the internet as their *Englisch* counterparts. If one saw him and the barn quilt and connected him with the Noah Frye who'd left Lancaster County after his wife's death, he and the *kinder* could be found. Letting his in-laws into their lives could endanger them again. He couldn't allow that.

Then he realized it was already too late. His eyes were caught by two people walking toward the gathering. They were still about halfway down the street, and he wouldn't have seen them if he hadn't been on the lift. Had they seen him? No, because they paused to look in a store window instead of rushing toward him, bringing the pain of the past with them.

He gripped the railing on the lift. What a *dummkopf* he was, worrying about social media! The damage had been done, and he had to do something, but what? He was committed to finishing at least another dozen barn quilts in the county. He couldn't. Finding someone to replace him wouldn't be difficult. All his successor needed to do was follow the patterns he'd marked. His gut twisted. How could he leave the barn quilt for the animal shelter undone? The Marquezes had done so much for him and Angela and Sam. He couldn't renege on his promise, but his first priority was protecting his son and daughter. He must get himself and his kids out of Lost River. He thought of the message from California that had arrived in the mail yesterday, a message he'd disregarded because he hadn't wanted to think about leaving Lost River.

Leaving Mollie.

God, he wanted to shout into the blue sky, *why did You offer me such happiness when You're making me choose between it and my* kinder*'s safety?*

It was quiet in Noah's studio later that afternoon. A rare thing and unsettling at the same time.

Every nerve Mollie had was jumping. She'd asked Noah yesterday if she could have two small leftover sections of the barn quilt boards, and he'd agreed. She'd set up a spot near the door where Angela and Sam could paint their own versions of the beautiful designs that flowed from their *daed*'s brush. She'd found shallow plastic bowls, and she'd put a small bit of paint in each one, cautioning the *kinder* not to splatter it.

The warning had been a waste of breath. Like their *daed*, they'd gotten paint all over the shirts she'd taken out of the mending box last week. Neither Tyler nor Kolton would miss the well-worn garments, and the shirts protected Angela's dress and Sam's trousers.

Their joy was in complete contrast to Noah. He was working as if his life depended on it on the barn quilt with the kitten peeking out from under the quilt.

What had happened in Lost River? She wasn't sure if she or the *kinder* had been more shocked when he'd bolted from the scissor lift before it'd stopped and led them away. At first, she'd guessed a persistent reporter had insisted on interviewing him, but he'd kept staring at the crowd. He'd increased their speed through the crowd, which was going in the opposite direction, toward where the carnival was about to open.

Who had spooked him?

Nobody had followed them, though lots of congratulations had been tossed in Noah's direction. At each one, he drew into himself as if the sound of his name was painful. He refused to answer her questions or the *kinder*'s as they got into the wagon and left the town behind. A thick cloud of dust had been raised in their wake as Noah pushed the horse to its top speed.

As they'd bounced over the uneven road, she had asked him what was wrong. He hadn't replied to her or to Angela and Sam when they asked when they were going to go to the carnival run by the firefighters to raise money for a new truck. She'd hushed the youngsters' questions, though her curiosity grew with each mile.

Noah had remained as reticent after they'd arrived back at the ranch. She'd waved to Daryn who was sitting on the bunkhouse porch, but Noah had acted as if the young man didn't exist. After striding to his studio, he'd opened the door and gone in without a backward look. As if he'd forgotten everything and everyone existed.

What *had* happened?

"Mollie!" Angela's insistent voice warned Mollie she'd been lost in thought for too long.

"What is it, *liebling*?" The endearment came naturally. "Are you done with your barn quilt?"

"Ja." She held it up. "See? It's *Daed* hanging his barn quilt." She pointed to a dark shape on a blue scissor lift in front of the bright red barn. "See? He's right there."

"What's this?" Mollie asked, pointing to a dark mass at the edge of the board.

"Those are the people watching him. If I could make a

painting with sound, you'd hear them cheering. Like today."
Her happy expression fell. "I wish we could have gone to
the carnival. Do you think we still can?"

"We'll have to see what your *daed* says."

"Will you ask him?"

Sam looked up. "Ask him, Mollie. He listens to you."

"He listens to you, too," she reassured the *kinder*.

Angela shook her head. "Not when he's like this."

"He's been like this before?" Mollie shouldn't be quizzing the *kinder* about their *daed* when he stood less than
twenty feet away, but her curiosity overruled her *gut* sense.

Sam said, "Before we left Wisconsin."

"And before we left Indiana," Angela added. "You don't
remember, Sam, because you were little, but he was like
this. Painting fast and not saying a word." Looking at Mollie, she said, "We can't be leaving here already. We just got
here. That can't be it, ain't so?"

Could a heart stop in the middle of a beat? Was Noah
truly getting ready to take his *kinder* and leave?

Chapter Thirteen

Noah took a deep breath when Mollie crossed his studio. He'd been trying to avoid talking to her since he'd rushed the *kinder* out of Lost River. If he opened his mouth, the wrong words might spill out. His temper had gotten the better of him in the past, and he wanted to be as composed as possible when he couldn't put off the conversation any longer.

He was furious. How could she have been so irresponsible?

Trying to calm himself, he knew he couldn't leave the barn quilt for the animal shelter unfinished. Losing himself in the bliss of painting should have given him the time he needed to tamp down his anger and his fear.

It hadn't done either, and he hadn't gotten far on the barn quilt. He wasn't doing much other than dabbing bits of color along the quilt to create what appeared to be small stitches in white thread.

Mollie stopped behind him. He didn't turn for a minute, then another, then a third. It was rude, he knew, but his fury boiled. He wasn't sure he could control it.

"Noah, I need to talk to you," she said.

"Can't you see I'm busy?" He didn't stop adding small lines of white across the bright red portion of the quilt. "Can't it wait?"

"No."

Noah froze at her scolding-teacher voice, then faced her. "If this is about going to attend the carnival…"

"It's not." Her low voice wouldn't reach the *kinder*. "Though you have two kids who'd like to go."

"Impossible! I've got to finish this before we go."

"Go? To the carnival or somewhere else?" She pushed on when his eyes narrowed. "I've been told you throw yourself into a work frenzy when you're moving on from a project. Are you finishing your part of the barn-quilt trail here?"

He put down the brush and walked around the tall board, out of the *kinder*'s view. When she followed, he said, "I saw them. In Lost River."

"Saw whom?"

"My in-laws." The words squeezed out between his clenched teeth like watermelon seeds.

"They're here?" Her eyes widened. "How did they find out you're here? I didn't think you corresponded with anyone they'd know."

"I didn't." His rage ricocheted through him like bolts of lightning. "There's only one way they could have found us so quickly. How could you break your word to me?"

"My word? About what?"

He clenched his fists by his sides, battling his bitterness, which was stronger than it'd been since he'd left Lancaster County. "I asked you not to write a word about Angela, Sam or me in your letters to *The Budget*."

"I haven't."

"Then how did they know we are here?"

"I don't know."

He heard the compassion and sorrow in her voice, but anger forced him to ignore both. His in-laws had always paged through the newspaper as soon as it was delivered, reading it from cover to cover. Once they had finished it, they discussed what they'd discovered, as if everyone mentioned in its pages were dearest friends. They prayed over mishaps and illnesses and deaths as well as celebrating family reunions and successful fundraisers. Funny stories brought laughter, as if they'd seen them firsthand.

"I don't know any other way they could have found out we were here," he snapped.

"I didn't write about you. If you don't believe me, check *The Budget*. You'll see my letters. They don't contain a single word about you and your family. They must have found you're here another way. You know the Amish grapevine is efficient."

He scowled. If simple gossip could have pinpointed his location to in-laws, Japheth and Jane Klingler, they would have found him years ago. They'd written to him after he'd taken the *kinder* away. He'd replied with a terse note and no return address. No more letters had reached him after his third move in less than a year. Betty Jane's parents hadn't had any way to trace him and his *kinder*. Not for the first time, Noah wished he'd changed his name and the *kinder*'s after they'd left Lancaster County. He'd worried that, though Angela was young, she'd reveal the truth.

When he didn't answer, Mollie wrung her hands together, then said, "Your in-laws are here, and—"

"I don't want them to find us."

Her eyebrows rose as her fingers stilled. "Why? They're your family. More important, they're Angela's and Sam's family. Their grandparents!"

"It doesn't matter. I must make sure our paths don't cross. You don't understand."

He was shocked when she grabbed his arm as he was about to turn away. Fighting his instinct to shake off her hand, he knew he could hurt her. Was that what he wanted? To make her feel as awful as he did?

"Then help me understand," she said, her voice even.

Staying calm was taking all her strength, he could tell. His own willpower wasn't up to the task of holding on to serenity. Rather, his mind was telling him to get out of the conversation before he said something he'd regret the moment the words left his lips.

"Mollie, this isn't your decision. It's mine, and I made it years ago. I don't want those people in my life or in my *kinder*'s lives."

"Why?" Her face fell, and tears blossomed in her eyes, but she held his gaze. She wasn't accusing him of anything. She didn't need to. He knew how many mistakes he'd made. He wasn't going to compound them.

"Because I can't forgive them for what happened."

"They saved your *kinder*!"

"But not my wife."

"Your *mamm*-in-law faced a horrible choice that day, Noah. A horrible, horrible choice I pray you and I will never have to face. She could save her *kind*, whom she loved, or your *kinder*, whom she loved. What would you have done if you'd been confronted by the same choice?"

He turned away, silent, so he didn't have to see her face to know accusations blazed on it. He'd seen the same expression on other faces. Faces he'd dared to believe belonged to friends who'd understand the depths of his loss and his grief and his anger at God and everyone in the world.

Everyone but his *kinder*.

"How can you be focused on the impossible and not be grateful for the possible?" Mollie demanded. "We can only do the best we can and pray it's enough."

"It wasn't enough. I know the truth. I can't trust anyone

else with my *kinder*." He saw her expectant look. She wanted to have him say he didn't trust anyone but her. He couldn't, though he wanted to. Saying those words would open his battered heart, releasing the flash flood of grief and pain and doubt he'd kept in there for half a decade.

She crossed her arms in front of her. "I never realized how selfish you are!"

"Selfish? I'm thinking of my family and—"

"'Doing what is best for them.' I know. I know." She raised her chin and met his gaze. Her words were cool, but the fire in her eyes seared him. "You say that, but you're selfish to deny yourself and your wife's family the chance for healing forgiveness."

"How can I forgive the unforgivable?"

"Because God asks us to. He asks us to forgive each other as He forgives us."

"That's easy for you to say because you don't remember who was involved when you were hurt." His pain lashed out at her, unstoppable. "Would you speak of forgiveness if you knew who'd done this to you?" He touched the scars on her cheeks.

When she jerked her head away, the small voice in his mind warned him he was destroying everything he'd found in the San Luis Valley, everything he'd discovered with Mollie, at the same he was tossing away everything his heart longed for. A new wave of rage washed over the cautioning words, silencing them.

"I don't know," she whispered, her voice breaking on each word.

"Until you know for sure, don't lecture me. I'm not one of your scholars!"

What are you doing? the little voice shouted, but that

bellow was silenced as pain threatened to steal every breath he took.

"No, you're not." Her answer was calm. Too calm because her tears fell. "Noah, how long are you going to wallow in grief and torture yourself with your memories? How long will you go on punishing yourself, punishing your family, punishing God? Until you drive everyone away, including Angela and Sam? Congratulations. You've succeeded in driving *me* away."

She didn't give him a chance to answer. Instead, she walked out of his studio. Not even his kids calling slowed her walk away from him.

It was just as well she hadn't waited for an answer because he didn't have one.

If anyone noticed Mollie was quiet at supper that evening, neither her brothers nor *Mamm* mentioned it. In fact, nobody spoke much. Did they have pressing matters on their minds as she did? Or were they looking forward to the tonight's entertainments to celebrate the Fourth?

It was hard to believe that only that morning, she'd been anticipating a *wunderbaar* day with Noah and the *kinder*. She'd been excited about everyone seeing Noah's hard work on the barn quilt. She'd planned to take Angela and Sam to the carnival after their picnic lunch. They would have enjoyed something from one of the food trucks for supper and ridden the Ferris wheel and the carousel before heading back to the ranch beneath the star-strewn sky.

Now, she was out of work. She wouldn't have the money to pay off the medical bills, but more important, she wouldn't be able to spend time with the *kinder*.

Or with Noah.

Her breath caught over her shredded heart, sending searing pain deep within her. She couldn't escape the replay of her final conversation with Noah while she cleared the table and put dishes in the sink. After *Mamm* left, going with Howard, Mollie assumed, to walk around the carnival and visit with friends, the words and high emotions between her and Noah pounded against her skull. Kolton went out to finish his chores, then came inside to change. The door closed behind her brothers, and the house grew silent, but her mind remained filled with memories of every minute she'd spent with Noah and his *kinder*.

Was this what Noah had endured for the past five years? The *what-ifs* and the *maybes* that refused to leave him alone?

She squeezed her eyes closed, but everything was inside her head, and it refused to be shut out. *God, did I do the wrong thing in leaving? Should I have been more understanding? Reacted less when he accused me of something I didn't do?*

Mollie sighed. She knew what God would expect of her. To forgive Noah and wish him the best in his search for whatever sanctuary he could find from his sorrow. If she knew where to begin...

With another sigh, she pulled her notebook out of a drawer and sat at the table to begin her next letter for *The Budget*. Her pen hung over the page, but no words came into her head. How could she write about today and not mention Noah? Did it matter any longer? She put down her pen, realizing for the first time since she'd taken over the job as a scribe that she had nothing to put in her letter to *The Budget*.

Jumping to her feet, Mollie grabbed her black bonnet off its peg and tied it under her chin. She couldn't stay in the house with her grim thoughts. It was less than a mile to Ruthanne's house, and at least a couple more hours of daylight were left before the sun vanished behind the San Juan Mountains. Hurrying along the deserted road, abutted on one side by a potato field, she made sure she stayed away from the edge of the asphalt. The drop into the drainage ditch was steep, and the vegetation growing in it was slippery with water from the irrigation system that arced across the field.

The blue house's door opened before she could reach it, and Ruthanne looked out. "Mollie! What are you doing here? I thought you'd be at the carnival."

"Can I *komm* in?" She hoped her friend would be a welcome distraction from her thoughts.

"*Ja*, but I'll be leaving in a few minutes." Ruthanne stepped back so Mollie could enter the kitchen with its once-white walls. The cabinets were beautiful, but two of the windows were cracked, and the ceiling was stained where water had dripped through it many years ago. "Albert and I are heading into Lost River for the carnival. Albert is determined to sample every food truck's wares before they close." She sat at the dark oak table. "Why aren't you with the Fryes?"

Mollie poured herself a glass of water, almost as at home in the Geers' kitchen as her own, because she'd spent so much time here since her childhood. Sitting across from her friend, she said, "I'm taking a break from watching Angela and Sam."

"A break?" Her friend's eyes narrowed. "Does this have anything to do with why you ran off this morning like you were rabbits with a wolf nipping your heels?"

"*Ja*." She tried to explain without revealing everything about Noah's past and his in-laws' appearance in Lost River. She could tell Ruthanne was confused, so she said, "He thinks I've got a big mouth and can't keep a promise."

"What sort of promise?" Ruthanne gasped. "Did he ask you to become the *mamm* for his *kinder*?"

"Don't be silly!" She gave a casual wave, but couldn't help noticing how her fingers trembled at the delicious thought of Noah professing his love for her and asking her to spend the rest of her life with him and his son and daughter. "Noah Frye isn't a frivolous man, and he's capable of taking care of Angela and Sam without anyone's help." She gave a laugh, or what she hoped sounded like a laugh. "Except when he's working, of course. Then he needs another set of eyes on them so they don't get into mischief."

"I don't understand what the problem is then."

"He asked me not to put anything in my *Budget* letters about him and his family. I agreed, but today, his in-laws came to the barn-quilt raising. That's why he wanted to get out of there fast."

"I don't understand."

Picking her words with care, Mollie said, "There's been trouble between Noah and his late wife's family, and it hasn't been resolved. He doesn't want to have it overshadow his life again. He can't figure out how anyone in Lancaster County in Pennsylvania could have known he and his *kinder* are in Lost River. That's why he believes I wrote something that pointed his in-laws in this direction."

"You didn't, ain't so?"

"Of course not!"

The sound of metal wheels announced a buggy was slowing in the yard. Ruthanne pushed herself to her feet. "That's Albert. Wait here."

"No, I should go. Albert has made it pretty clear he doesn't want to spend time with me."

"Don't be absurd. We're your friends, and it'll do him

gut to talk about plans for the wedding." She put her hand on Mollie's arm. "It'll do you *gut*, too."

Though the last thing Mollie wanted to talk about was a wedding when Noah had shoved her aside, she nodded. She'd stay for a few minutes, then excuse herself so Ruthanne and Albert could be on their way to the carnival. It wasn't her friend's problem that Mollie had fallen in love with a man who didn't trust her. It was hers.

And hers alone.

That word—*alone*—had never been so absolute.

Chapter Fourteen

Noah looked up, hope leaping into his throat as he heard footsteps outside his studio. Could Mollie be returning to allow them to patch over the hateful words spoken in the heat of their conversation?

Angela's and Sam's heads rose, too. He saw his wish on their young faces. Shame dropped on him. When he'd lambasted Mollie, accusing her of betraying them, he hadn't stopped to think how his *kinder* would feel when they learned she wasn't returning. His thoughts—scanty while suffocated by his anger—had been focused solely on himself. As they'd been when he vanished from Lancaster County in the middle of the night, so desperate to flee his grief he didn't consider what his choice would mean to anyone else in the coming days, weeks, years.

He stared at Jerek, who walked into his studio with Carlos and a female police officer. The bishop glanced at the *kinder*, then said, "Carlos, I see two youngsters who'd love to sample your empanadas that smell so *gut.*"

"Empanadas and sweet plantains. Yummy!" Carlos's enthusiasm was as forced as Jerek's, and Noah guessed the bishop had something he wanted to discuss that he didn't want the *kinder* to overhear.

"Save some for me." The words almost stuck in Noah's

gullet, but Angela and Sam didn't notice as they rushed to the door and left with Carlos.

"This is Officer Flores," Jerek said. "She's got news to share with you."

"About the attempted destruction of my barn quilt?" He couldn't imagine another reason a cop and the local bishop would come to talk to him.

The woman, who was almost as tall as he was, nodded. "Along with what was done to your studio." She glanced around, though there was nothing left of the damage to see.

Mollie had worked hard to get the space clean so no reminders would upset the *kinder*. Or him. Something else she'd done for him without being asked. He was slowly realizing how much she'd touched every facet of his life.

"I wanted to let you know, Mr. Frye—"

He interrupted her. "Noah, please."

"I wanted you to know, Noah, our investigation turned up a young man and woman who have confessed to the crime."

"Who?" he asked, steeling himself for hearing plain names.

"Lacey and Brant Hunter, Junior."

He mouthed their names, but no sound came from his mouth.

The bishop nodded. "They're the oldest *kinder* of Brant Hunter."

"The chairman of the arts council," Carlos said as he reentered the studio.

Noah wondered who was watching Angela and Sam, and Carlos confirmed he'd left them with his wife, who was going to take them out to see the new ponies. Trying not to obsess about having the kids out of his sight, he asked, "Why would Brant's *kinder* wreck my studio and my work?"

"Because Brant asked them to." Carlos's voice was as cold as a winter morning.

Listening in disbelief, Noah didn't want to believe what Officer Flores shared with him. The teens had confessed, not wanting to take the rap alone. When confronted, Brant had talked.

"It was simple," the police officer said. "He was in favor of the project at the beginning, but then he began to believe he was getting shown up by his vice chair."

"Wendy Warner," Carlos said, as if Noah could forget the abrasive woman. "Brant began to think prestige would pass him by. He panicked because he wants to run for political office, and he'd counted on the project being his ticket to winning."

"He also sent a note to you to get you out of the studio," Jerek said, "and to turn suspicion on Wendy."

"He's admitted this?" Noah asked, astonished.

"Enough." Officer Flores gave him a nod, then said, "We don't need anything further right now, Mr.— Noah. If we do, we'll alert Bishop Stahl."

Noah thanked the officer. After she'd left, Noah was grateful Carlos and Jerek stayed. He bowed his head as the bishop offered a prayer for the Hunter family and the healing of their unhappy hearts. Though he didn't mention anyone else's heart, Noah hoped the bishop was including Noah's battered heart in the prayer. It had a lot of healing to do…and he needed to start with Mollie.

"I don't want to."

Mollie listened in disbelief as she heard Albert Wynes's voice. It was deeper than she recalled, and not even Sam on his worst day whined like that. Pain speared her as she realized how much she already missed the Frye *kinder*.

Would she ever see Noah and his family again? Her heart broke anew.

"Albert, it's *gut* to see you," Mollie said with the best enthusiasm she could muster when Ruthanne walked inside with her fiancé, their shadows growing long as the sun headed toward the western horizon.

He hung his head. "I don't know why you'd say that."

Mollie glanced at Ruthanne, who shrugged. Was Albert so averse to being in the same room with her?

"Stop being such a grump." Ruthanne's smile faltered as her gaze caught Mollie's. "Sit and be patient while I talk with Mollie."

He muttered something and dropped into a chair by the black woodstove in a corner of the kitchen, farthest from where Mollie stood.

Ruthanne said, "Forgive him. He's been in a bad mood for days. He won't explain why, and I'm tired of asking him what's wrong." Her voice grew gentler. "What can I do to help you and Noah?"

"There's no Noah and me."

"He's hurt you, ain't so?" Ruthanne took Mollie's hands and squeezed them. "Are you sure he meant it?" She shot a glance over her shoulder. "Sometimes we say things we don't mean."

Albert grumbled, "Can we go?"

His fiancée ignored him. "Mollie, I know how much you care about him and the *kinder*. What did he do that has hurt you so much? It's more than insisting you broke a promise to him, ain't so?"

She wanted to say that was enough to drive her away, but her heart refused to let her. It wasn't the truth. The words burst from her. "He told me I shouldn't lecture him about forgiving his in-laws, because I didn't understand what it was to be haunted by memories." She touched her right cheek. "He acted as if my amnesia was a blessing."

"It is!" shouted Albert as he jumped to his feet. "You don't have to relive that night over and over, never able to change a single thing that happened."

Mollie stared at him. "You were there that night?"

"Who else do you think was driving? You?" he sneered. "You were the *gut* girl, the one who always obeyed the rules. I wouldn't trust you with my buggy."

"*You* were driving the buggy?" she asked, shocked as she heard Ruthanne's gasp. "Why haven't you told me?"

"I thought you knew." His voice remained defensive, and he refused to meet her eyes. "You're the smartest one, spouting off facts and figures the rest of us have forgotten. You remember everything."

She struggled to reply. "You know that's not true, Albert. You know I've lost my memories of that night and for several weeks afterward."

"I wasn't sure which ones you'd lost."

"I lost all of them. You know that!" She gave a terse laugh. "Or you would have if you'd bothered to ask me. Everyone else checked in with me to make sure I was okay. You didn't, ain't so?"

"I knew you've lost some memories, but not which ones."

Before Mollie could respond to his evasive remarks, Ruthanne ordered, "Stop it, Albert! Be honest with Mollie." Her voice broke. "Be honest with me."

He hung his head as he sat again. He kneaded his fingers together between his knees. "I never meant for anyone to get hurt, Ruthanne. You've got to believe me."

"I'm not sure what to believe, Albert." Ruthanne's voice was strained. "I can't believe you've kept this truth hidden from me. I've told you my best friend has been hurt because her memories had vanished."

"I thought I was your best friend. I—" He halted when Ruthanne fired a glare at him. Lowering his head once more, he muttered, "It wasn't anything anyone planned. We were going to have fun."

"With buggy races?" asked Mollie. Though she couldn't believe—had never believed—she would have been part of such a dangerous sport, she needed to have the truth confirmed…at last.

When Albert didn't answer, Ruthanne demanded, "Were you racing buggies when Mollie was hurt?"

"Not exactly."

Again, Mollie's astonishment kept her silent. And again, it was Ruthanne who asked the question shrieking in her head, "What do you mean 'not exactly?'"

"We saw a video. Someone had a carriage that looked like it was drifting."

"Drifting?" asked Mollie and Ruthanne at the same time, then Mollie added, "What's that?"

"Drifting is when you turn a vehicle at a sharp angle while going at a high speed. Auto racers do it. The back wheels slide, making the vehicle appear to be going sideways and forward at the same time." Albert cleared his throat as if each word was harder to speak than the previous one. "We decided to try it."

"Who is *we*?" Ruthanne asked. "You and Mollie decided to do that?"

Mollie wanted to shout she wouldn't have done such a thing, but how did she know? So much had been wiped from her head, refusing to be recovered, but one memory burst out like a jack-in-the-box. She could remember lying on the cold road and hearing frenzied voices, but nobody spoke to her or came near. Pain seared her whole right side, centering along her face. Something sticky had clung to her, and it took her a long time to realize it was her own blood. When had the voices vanished, abandoning her? That answer refused to appear, but *Mamm* had said Mollie must have been there for several hours before someone passed by and called the police.

"I should have said," Albert answered, "*I* decided to try it. Folks claimed you could make a buggy drift if the roads were slick. I wanted to try it because we'd had a big rainstorm and the roads hadn't dried. I never imagined a car would come along. I was so intent on creating the skid I didn't notice the car's lights until it was too late." Tears flooded his eyes. "I'm sorry, Mollie. I shouldn't have put you in peril. I should have let you out of the buggy when you asked me to. You'd been such a *gut* friend to me. I wish I'd been as *gut* a friend to you."

"Why didn't you help me after the accident?" Mollie asked, desperate to learn everything about that night.

"I was scared. I got my horse and buggy out of there. I figured you'd be okay to walk home."

"You didn't check on her?" Ruthanne's fury exploded out in those words.

He shook his head. "You know I don't like blood."

Ruthanne strode to the door and opened it. "Leave, Albert."

"Are you sure?" he asked as he stood. "We can still go to the carnival."

"You waited too many years to tell the truth, but I'll tell you the truth right now. I'm not going anywhere with you again. Not as your friend and not as your wife. Leave, and don't *komm* back."

Mollie stared in disbelief as Albert obeyed. How could

he walk out without trying to hold on to his love for her friend? *How could* you *walk out on the love you had for Noah?* retorted her conscience. She pressed her hand over her heart, knowing she should have stood up for herself as she'd stood up for her scholars and family. Was it too late? Another question she couldn't answer.

Before Ruthanne shut the door behind Albert, she called after him, "Don't darken my doorstep again, Albert Wynes!" She slammed the door, but her shoulders shook with grief and betrayal.

"Go after him," Mollie urged. "You love Albert. You want to marry him. This shouldn't change anything."

Ruthanne grasped her hands as the sound of the buggy leaving filtered into the house. "It changes everything. I would never have agreed to be his wife if I'd known what he'd done and how he'd lied about it. To everybody, including me."

"Don't let one mistake lead to another." Her voice caught on the words she'd wanted to say to Noah.

"Albert could have told me the truth long ago, and I would have listened and not judged him. Everyone can be feckless at one time or another." She shook her head. "I've been a *dummkopf* while planning a wedding it's clear Albert didn't want. A part of me has known that for a while, but I didn't want to believe it." Tears welled into her eyes, but they didn't fall. "It's like I'm waking from a nightmare I didn't know I was having."

Mollie offered to stay with her friend and talk longer, but Ruthanne insisted she wasn't going to let breaking up with Albert keep her from the carnival. She asked Mollie to go, but Mollie declined. The idea of being around happy parents and *kinder* was too much for her fragile heart.

Telling Ruthanne to have a *gut* time, she headed along

the road toward her empty house. Her shadow stretched far in front of her, but nothing else moved along the road, which was bordered on the right side by a field of potatoes. The giant irrigation system was, for once, unmoving, though water flowed in the ditch next to the road.

"Help!"

Mollie stopped. Had her ears deceived her? Had it been a soft cry for help, or was it a bird's call?

"Help! Mollie, help!"

She stared in horror at the drainage ditch. Angela! Sam!

She raced toward where the two *kinder* were struggling to climb out, but kept sliding back in. For a moment, she was puzzled because they should have been able to scramble out of the water and onto the road. Then she saw their left arms were hanging at strange angles. Broken?

She prayed not. Hoping no snakes or other creatures lurked in the murky bottom of the ditch, she splashed to the *kinder* as they cried out her name over and over in obvious pain.

Though she wanted to ask what they were doing in a ditch they knew was dangerous, she focused on assisting them. It was simplest to stand in the bottom of the ditch and lift them onto the asphalt.

"Stay close to the edge," she warned, "and watch out for vehicles!"

They didn't reply, which worried her more. When she saw tears of pain on their faces, she began to pray they weren't badly hurt.

On her hands and knees, she crawled out of the ditch and squatted beside the *kinder*. They were wet and filthy, their clothes torn and stained with mud and bits of leaves. Had they crossed the mile-wide field on their own?

"What hurts?" she asked, pushing aside other questions. "Just your arms?"

Angela nodded at the same time Sam shook his head.

"Let me check," she said gently as the *kinder* continued to sob.

Angela winced as she lowered her right hand, which was supporting her left arm. With a gasp and a big sob, she clutched her arm in her hand again.

Mollie put one hand under the little girl's arm as she ran her other one along it. She couldn't keep from wincing herself when she discovered the break in at least one bone of Angela's forearm. After pulling off her apron, she strained to rip it in half. She wrapped one half around the tiny arm, hoping it would stabilize the bone and prevent further injury.

Angela moaned, and Mollie said, "I'm sorry. I know it hurts."

"It does. Really, really bad."

"I'll be careful."

She thought Angela would keep arguing, but the little girl must have been in too much pain to continue. She let Mollie tie off the apron and sat while Mollie repeated the whole procedure with Sam's left arm.

"You've broken your arm, I think, *liebling*."

Sam held his arm close to his chest, not willing to chance being hurt more. Neither he nor his sister made any sense when Mollie asked them how they'd fallen into the ditch, so she gave up trying to get answers from them. Instead, she stood and saw a tractor coming along the otherwise deserted road.

When Mollie flagged down the farmer, he took one look at the drenched *kinder* and handed her his phone. She dialed 911 and asked for an ambulance to transport Sam and Angela to the hospital in Del Norte, a town northwest of Lost River. The farmer offered to stay with them while they waited, but she thanked him for his kindness in stopping and the bottle of water he left with them.

She began to wonder if she'd been wrong to return the phone because time passed as if moving through thickening mud. The 911 operator had asked her to stay on the line, but she hadn't wanted to delay the farmer from getting home when a thunderstorm was brewing to the west.

She sat between the two youngsters and offered the water bottle first to one and then to the other. Having them get dehydrated would make their situation more perilous. She held the bottle to their lips because she didn't want them shifting their arms.

"Does your *daed* know where you are?" she asked when they'd calmed a bit.

"No," said Angela softly.

"We…" Sam winced as if it hurt to say a single word. He blinked more tears before he added, "We left him a note."

"What did your note say?" she asked.

"We wanted to see you," Sam answered.

"We thought you'd know where we could pick columbines for him," Angela added. "He's been sad, and we thought flowers would make him not sad any longer."

It was Mollie's turn to wince. Angela hadn't said her *daed* would be happy with the flowers. Only not sad.

"We want you to *komm* back," the little boy said.

"Sam!" Angela glanced at Mollie. "You know *Daed* doesn't want us to talk about that."

"With him!" Sam frowned. "He didn't say we couldn't talk about it with Mollie."

"You know what he means."

"He means we're going to leave, and we're not going to see her again. I don't want not to see her again." New tears burst from the *kind*.

As his sister sobbed with him, Mollie heard a siren. Thanking God the ambulance was on its way, she made sure the youngsters were off the road, but away from the ditch, when the vehicle slowed in front of them.

The EMTs examined both kids, then put them into the rear. Motioning for Mollie to join them, they jumped in as well. The driver headed north while Mollie shared what scant information she had. The taller EMT assured her she could call the Marquezes' ranch from the hospital. She nodded, not wanting to think how frantic Noah must be with his *kinder* missing.

Mollie stepped to one side as the kids were wheeled into the emergency room. She'd been in the hospital so many times when her *daed* had gone in the futile attempt to defeat his cancer, but she'd never visited the emergency room.

An intake nurse took what information she had. Once the nurse learned Mollie wasn't the youngsters' *mamm*, she arranged with a volunteer to contact the ranch. Mollie and the *kinder* were instructed to go to the waiting area. A low hum of activity buzzed around the rows of chairs where sick and injured people and their loved ones sat waiting for their turn to be seen.

On either side of her, Noah's *kinder* whimpered. She thought of the times they'd skinned their knees or elbows or been scratched by Mariposa. Not a tear had been shed then. They must be in great pain.

She tried not to imagine what Noah was feeling. Sam had left him a note, but the two kids were young, and their spelling was rudimentary at best. Had Noah been able to decipher it? If he did, was he on his way to her house? Nobody was there, and the call to the ranch might take time to reach him. In the meantime, he'd be wild with worry.

It seemed like an eternity, but it must have been no more

than fifteen minutes before a dark-haired young man wearing bright blue scrubs called out, "Angela and Samuel Frye."

"Here." Mollie raised her hand, then realized she looked silly. Helping the youngsters stand, she led them to where the nurse waited.

He looked at the papers he held, then asked, "Are you their mother?"

"No."

"I'm afraid you can't come with them."

"I'm their nanny." Or at least she had been before Noah had fired her.

You're not being fair, her conscience retorted. *He didn't fire you. You quit.*

"I'm sorry," the nurse said as he stepped aside while two wheelchairs were brought. "Only immediate family."

"They need someone with them!"

"Their father has been called. Until he arrives, a patient-care tech will stay with them."

Wanting to argue it might be an hour or more before Noah got the message and found a ride to the hospital, Mollie nodded. She leaned down to where Sam and Angela were slouched in the wheelchairs. "You're going with this nice nurse." She glanced at the man's name tag. "With Santiago. He and the other nurses and *doktors* will make sure you're taken care of."

"Want you, Mollie," groaned Sam.

"*Komm* with us, Mollie." Angela clutched Mollie's skirt with her *gut* hand.

"I'll be there as soon as I can." It was a promise she hoped she could keep.

She winced as she heard the *kinder*'s frightened cries as they were rolled away by strangers. Sympathetic glances in her direction didn't ease how Sam's and Angela's yells echoed. She dropped to her chair and hid her face in her hands.

For the next hour, while a storm thundered outside, Mollie sat alone. There were other people in the waiting area, but she ignored them, cocooned in her own distress. Each time someone emerged from the treatment area, she looked up, hopeful, though she doubted they'd release the *kinder* to anyone but their *daed.*

She bent her head and thanked God for letting her be in the right place at the right time to help. Albert's confession hadn't resurrected any missing memories except for the feeling of being left alone by the side of the road, lost in pain and covered with her own blood. She'd kept the *kinder* from suffering that.

The doors to the parking lot opened every few minutes, but strangers entered each time. When Noah finally walked through, his face long with fear, she started to rise, but he was swept away by a lady in a pink coat as soon as he mentioned his name.

Sitting, Mollie realized for the first time she had no idea how she was going to get home. It was more than twenty miles. She went to look out the window, hoping to see either Carlos's or *Doktor* Lynny's truck.

"Miss Lehman?"

Mollie whirled to see a nurse about her age. The redhead wore a name tag that read *Bette.*

"Would you like to see the children, Miss Lehman?" Bette asked.

"Ja!"

"Come with me." The nurse's smile broadened. "They've been asking for you, and their father agreed for you to see them so they wouldn't be so agitated."

Dismay pinched her heart. Had Noah agreed for her to

see the *kinder* only because they were upset? She'd hoped he would want to see her, too.

Bette drew aside a striped curtain, and Mollie edged forward into the room with two empty beds. Her eyes riveted on the man setting himself on his feet.

Noah's face was drawn. His clothes were filthy, and she wondered if he'd tried to follow the kids through the fields. Had he traipsed through an irrigation ditch, too? His hair was laced with leaves and twigs, and a bruise was darkening his right cheek. It took every ounce of her self-control to keep from brushing the debris from his hair.

"Where are Sam and Angela?" she asked.

"In the cast room." He shifted uneasily.

"How are they doing?"

"Not happy."

"I'm sure their arms hurt a lot."

He gave her a wry smile, and her heart tugged. "They started doing okay as soon as the nurses told them they could have any color cast they want." His expression grew somber again. "They're not happy with me, but I'm sure you know that."

"I'm a teacher, Noah. As I've told you before, I heed what upset *kinder* say with a grain of salt."

"Gut." He didn't add anything else.

She locked her hands behind her so she didn't grasp his arms and shake him while she asked why he was treating her like a stranger. He'd been right. It was so much harder to deal with the past when you recalled every detail than it was if the memories had been swept away. She knew this memory would stalk her forever.

Chapter Fifteen

Had he been wrong to let the staff bring Mollie to the treatment room? Noah rubbed his hands together as he looked at the curtain, willing it to be pushed aside and his *kinder* returned to him. Focusing on them should keep him from thinking about Mollie, who was standing on the far side of the empty beds. He wasn't comfortable talking to her after their explosive last conversation.

After she'd left, he'd pulled the letter he'd gotten the day before out of the trash. It asked him to consider a job establishing another barn quilt trail near Lake Tahoe, the third such letter he'd received in as many days. He'd dismissed it, but now reread it. He'd finished the barn quilt for the animal shelter and had been packing his few belongings—with the offer secure at the bottom of his bag—and the *kinder*'s, when Angela and Sam had vanished. *Doktor* Lynny had been called to the phone and had left the youngsters in her kitchen with cookies. When she returned less than five minutes later, they were gone. She'd alerted Noah, and he knew where they'd gone. To tell Mollie goodbye. He'd headed to her house at top speed. Nobody had been home, so he'd decided to try the school. No one there, either. Driving into Lost River and wandering through the carnival had been futile. He'd returned to the ranch to discover Carlos searching for *him* with news from the hospital.

Now, he stood with Mollie, who'd found his *kinder* and gotten them to the emergency room. As if nothing had changed.

But it had.

He cut his eyes to her. She looked disheveled but lovely. The concern in her eyes was genuine, he knew. Just as his longing to cross the room and sweep her into his arms was real.

Except he was leaving. Tonight, if possible, before panic strangled him.

The curtain was pushed aside again, and his kids returned on a single gurney. Their tears had been dried, and their faces washed. The torn pieces of Mollie's apron had been replaced with casts. A brilliant pink one encased Angela's left wrist while high-vis green swathed Sam's lower arm. They smiled around the lollipops they had in their mouths when they saw who was waiting for them.

"Mollie, look!" Angela cried. "Isn't it pretty?"

"Not as pretty as your healed arm will be when the cast is removed," she answered.

"Sign mine first!" Sam held up his arm, then paused and took a lick of his lollipop before he asked, "What does 'sign it' mean?"

"Did the nurse tell you about that?" she asked, smiling. "It means you can ask friends and family to write their names on your cast. Sort of a get-well card you carry around with you."

"Can Mollie put her name on my cast first, *Daed*?" Angela asked.

As always when his daughter had an idea, his son added, "Me, too!"

Mollie looked at him, and he could not keep from meeting her compassionate gaze. If he said no, she would have found a way to explain *his* reaction to *his* kids in a wise and gentle way.

A warmth he hadn't expected to feel again rushed from his heart to his toes. His *kinder* had been furious when he hadn't stopped Mollie from leaving. Though he hadn't guessed they'd take matters into their own small hands, he'd learned how strong their connection was to her.

And his?

Noah focused on the conversation in front of him so he could ignore his uncomfortable thoughts. Mollie was examining the casts as if she'd never seen anything so interesting in her whole life. When Angela and Sam showed her the coloring books and stickers they'd been given to take home, guilt speared him again. What did his kids know about home? A real home? He been dragging them from one place to another since Betty Jane's death.

"If you want to sign the casts, Mollie, go ahead," he said.

"I'd like to." She lowered her voice so it reached only his ears. "I'd like them to have something to remember me by."

"Mollie…"

"Ja?" she asked when his voice faded away.

He couldn't answer her as the curtain opened again. Every word he'd known fled from his brain as he stared at the two people framed by the doorway. When he'd seen them in Lost River, he'd taken one quick look. For the first time in five years, he looked directly at his in-laws.

Japheth Klingler's hair was grayer, and his beard reached farther down his chest. Otherwise, time had had little effect on him. The same couldn't be said for his wife. Jane's hair was as white as the snow clinging to the peaks of the distant mountains. Deep lines had carved arroyos in her cheeks and across her brow. Her shoulders were hunched, as if she carried a vast burden.

She did, he knew. She hadn't been able to save her own *kind*, having to choose between her *kins-kinder* and her daughter. What had Mollie said before she walked out of his studio? The words were etched on his brain.

Your mamm-*in-law faced a horrible choice that day, Noah. A horrible, horrible choice I pray you and I will never have to face. She could save her* kind, *whom she loved, or your* kinder, *whom she loved. What would you have done if you'd been confronted by the same choice?*

For the first time, he wasn't sure.

As she'd done so often since he arrived on her doorstep in error, Mollie saved Noah by breaking the silence. "Are you Noah's family?"

His *daed*-in-law nodded and shared their names as he and Jane stared at the *kinder* with avid longing.

Aware of the *kinder* listening, Noah knew he should say something, but his mouth was frozen shut.

Again, Mollie spared him from embarrassment. "I'm Mollie Lehman." She offered them a warm smile. "I was Angela and Sam's teacher after they arrived in Lost River, but during the summer break, I've been watching them while Noah paints." Without giving Noah a chance to speak, she faced his kids. "Angela, Sam, these are your *grossmammi* and your *grossdawdi*."

"We've got a *grossmammi* and a *grossdawdi*?" asked Angela as she looked from Mollie to Betty Jane's parents and then to him. "*Daed*, is this true?"

"Mollie wouldn't tell you anything but the truth, ain't so?" he answered, glad his mouth had begun to function.

"When we heard people talking in Lost River about two plain *kinder* who'd been brought to the hospital," Jane said softly, "we hurried here, hoping our *kins-kinder* weren't the ones everyone was talking about."

"How did other people hear?" Noah asked.

Chuckling, Mollie said, "There are a lot of scanners in the valley. Because we're so spread out, people like to listen to calls for emergencies so they know what's going on." Without giving him a chance to respond, she went on, "Angela and Sam are going to be fine." Mollie smiled at his kids. "They've each got a broken bone, but isn't that a normal part of being a *kind*? No matter how much we try to protect them, sometimes we can't. That's why we have to trust in God to watch over us, ain't so?"

The question was aimed at him, Noah knew. He'd expected his *mamm*-in-law to protect his family as if she was God. That hadn't been fair. *What would you have done if you'd been confronted by the same choice?* It wasn't a decision anyone could make without second-guessing themselves for the rest of their life. Seeing the furrows in Jane's face as if for the first time, he knew that his leaving had added to the pain and self-accusations that had tormented her for years.

Noah moved around Mollie so he could stand face-to-face with his wife's parents. It's where he should have stood five years ago instead of heaping fault on them and running in the opposite direction.

When Japheth put a steadying hand on his wife's arm, Noah wondered how much needless pain he'd caused.

"I should have said this a long time ago," he said, surprised how easily the words rolled off his lips. *God, danki for giving me the courage to speak the truth.* "I don't blame you for Betty Jane's death, Japheth. Nor you, Jane. I blamed myself."

"That's nonsense," Japheth said. "You were cutting hay when the fire began."

"I believed I should have been there to protect my family." He put a hand on Jane's bent shoulder. "Now, with *kinder* of my own, I know I can't shield them from danger every minute of every day. It was an impossible task I expected you to do. I didn't see that at the time—or until now—because I was drowning in my grief. I refused to open my eyes to see I wasn't alone in sorrow. Forgive me for refusing to realize that then and since."

He held his breath as no one spoke. Had he waited too long to express the words he'd kept bottled up in his heart? The words that would help heal.

"We've missed you and the *kinder*, son." Japheth's smile was unsteady. "Could we talk to our *kins-kinder*?"

Sam held out his arm with the cast. "Sign it?"

Everyone laughed, and Noah watched his in-laws chat with his kids, getting to know them. He saw Mollie smiling by the curtain, but didn't have a chance to speak to her before a nurse came in with a stack of papers. The nurse asked him to come with her so she could explain what care the casts would need and have him sign the necessary paperwork. Herding him out of the treatment area, she led him to a counter. The stack was higher than he'd expected. He was given a copy of everything and told he could take the *kinder* home.

Pulling out the cell phone Carlos had lent him, he started to call his host to arrange a ride to the ranch. A woman stopped him and pointed to the sign that said all calls must be made in the waiting room. He hurried out, made the call and returned to collect his family. He picked up Angela while Japheth cradled Sam in his arms. For the first time, Noah could see a resemblance between his *kinder* and their grandparents. He knew Betty Jane would be pleased with tonight's events, and he was glad he could make the most important woman in his life five years ago happy one more time.

If he could make the most important woman in his life *now* happy, he—

"Where's Mollie?" asked Angela.

He looked around, shocked. Where *was* she?

"If you're talking about the teacher," Jane said, "she left a few minutes ago. She said to tell you goodbye and that you'd understand why she had to go."

Noah's knees threatened to collapse beneath him. Mollie had left without saying anything to him? Maybe she'd said everything she'd had to say when he'd accused her of betraying him.

"Japheth," he began. He needed to know the truth as much as he needed his next breath. "How did you learn we were in Lost River?"

"Jane told me." He looked at his wife. "How did you hear Noah and the *kinder* were in Colorado?"

"Someone at church mentioned it, but I don't know how they knew. We decided to take a chance and see if the rumor was true."

His head reeled. What a *dummkopf* he was! As he was beginning to heal one wound he'd caused, he had created another.

He wasn't sure if he'd be given the chance to repair it.

Noah stopped the wagon in front of the Lehmans' house three evenings later, then pulled it into the drive that led around to the barns. Beside him, Angela and Sam sat in silence. In fact, they hadn't said a single word on the ride from the ranch to the small farm. They'd been having such fun with their grandparents before he'd said they needed to do an important errand. The *kinder* had lost their smiles, and their shoulders had drooped.

Did they dread this visit as much as he did? He had no idea why Mollie had sent a note requesting that he and the youngsters stop by her house tonight after supper. When the message had been delivered and he'd seen it was from her, he'd been ecstatic. The curt invitation to the house hadn't offered any way to bridge the chasm he'd opened between them. Did she want to explain, after three days, why she'd left the hospital without a word?

He helped the *kinder* out of the wagon, taking care not to bump their casts that were growing grungy where they weren't covered with the names of everyone they met.

Everyone but Mollie.

As if he'd spoke aloud, Sam asked, "Will Mollie sign it?"

"Let's see." He didn't want to make any promises he couldn't keep. He flinched at the thought. Even before Betty Jane's parents had assured him they hadn't found out about the Fryes being in Lost River from *The Budget*, he'd known he had wronged Mollie with his accusations.

Noah's hopes for an easy encounter vanished when Mollie opened the door. Dark arcs under her eyes suggested she hadn't slept since he last saw her at the hospital. The bright sparkle in her eyes had dimmed like an extinguished candle. She was wearing a new, crisp black apron over her dark green dress to replace the one she'd ripped apart to protect his kids' arms.

"We're here to say goodbye." Angela threw her arms around Mollie before anyone else spoke. "I don't want to say goodbye."

Drawing her away, Noah wondered how one small girl with only one usable arm could hold on as tight as a leech.

He peeled her away in time for Sam to throw himself forward, and babble something Noah couldn't understand. He didn't need to know the words. His son believed they were there to say farewell as Angela did.

"We're here because Mollie wants to speak with us," Noah said.

"Me?" Mollie asked in the same toneless voice.

He gave her a puzzled frown. "You asked us to visit."

"I didn't." Her icy demeanor cracked, but the joy that had bloomed on her face was gone. He knew he was the one who'd banished it.

"I got a note saying I should stop by this evening." He looked at the *kinder* by his side. "That we should stop by."

"I didn't send it. I'd thought you'd left Lost River."

A motion caught his eye. Ruthanne Geer stepped out of the living room and moved to stand beside Mollie. Her pose stated without a single word that she was there to protect her friend. From him? He ached to reassure both women he'd never do anything to hurt Mollie, but he had.

"She didn't send the note," Ruthanne said. "I did."

"You did?" asked Mollie at the same time he did.

Ruthanne nodded. "Mollie, your *mamm* made banana-carrot cake, ain't so? You mentioned there was some left."

He deciphered the glance Mollie's friend gave her. Ruthanne wanted to be able to speak without the *kinder* overhearing. Nothing would distract his youngsters like one of Viola's sweet treats. Within minutes, Angela and Sam were seated at the kitchen table with cake and glasses of *millich*. Ruthanne led the way out to the front porch.

As soon as the door was closed, she said, "Noah, you were upset when your late wife's parents arrived. So upset you blamed Mollie for revealing where you and the *kinder* are."

"I did." He sighed. "I made a mistake. A huge mistake."

He tried to capture Mollie's gaze, but she stared across the road at the fields stretching toward the western mountains, her fingertips on her cheek as if she could hide the scars. Wishing he could speak to her alone, he realized Ruthanne wasn't going to leave while he was there.

"It was a whopper of a mistake," Ruthanne said, firing back.

"Ruthanne..." Mollie began.

He didn't let her finish. She shouldn't be scolding her friend. He was the one who'd made a complete mess of everything, listening to guilt that had pleaded with him to ignore the truth. If he'd listened to his heart... Mollie was right when she'd said he'd forgotten how to do that.

"I had no reason to believe she had broken that promise," he said.

"You're right!" Ruthanne stuck her fists on her hips. "When she told me about your false accusations, I believed her—she hadn't broken her promise. Why couldn't you believe her, too? She'd never do anything to hurt someone else, especially someone she loves as much as she loves you and your *kinder*."

Mollie drew in a sharp breath at the same moment his heart hammered against his ribs. Hearing that she loved him—even when spoken in anger by her friend—tore away the last illusion he'd created as meticulously as he had the barn quilts. He'd hid behind it, not willing to show his real face and his real heart, too afraid of having his life shredded again.

Ruthanne wasn't finished. "You're blaming the wrong person, Noah. If you feel you have to find someone to fault, it's me."

"You?" asked Mollie, amazement raising her voice.

"Ja." She took her friend's hands, but her words were

for Noah. "After you told me about what had happened, it got me thinking, Mollie. I wanted to think about something other than kicking Albert to the curb."

Noah looked at Mollie, unsure what Ruthanne meant. When she mouthed, *Later*, he nodded.

"I mentioned to *Mamm*," Ruthanne continued, "you and the *kinder* had arrived here, Noah. At first, I wrote to her that you were from the Midwest, then I heard you were from Lancaster County." She held up a single hand to halt his reply. "No, Mollie didn't share that with me. It was something Carrie said because she recognized your accent. Her family is from Pennsylvania as well."

He nodded, recalling how the young woman had talked about her relatives in Somerset County. When he'd told her about attending one of their services as part of his youth group's long-distance outing, Carrie must have realized he'd lived in either Pennsylvania or Maryland. He wondered how many other ways he'd given himself away without realizing it.

"When I wrote to *Mamm* about how Carrie recognized you were from Pennsylvania," Ruthanne went on, "she must have spoken about how far you've traveled when talking with my sister's neighbors in Lancaster County. They asked her to ask me if you were the Noah Frye who once lived in East Earl."

"You couldn't have answered that," Mollie said.

She lowered her eyes. "I didn't have to, because forgive me, Noah, but I'd shared your *kinder*'s names with *Mamm* because I know how much she enjoys stories about young ones' antics. She must have told my sister's neighbors, and they put two and two together. They guessed you had to be the man who'd left the area after a tragic fire at his farm five years ago."

"One of them told my in-laws." He didn't bother to make it a question. He could imagine how fast the news had spread across the rolling hills, and how many people discovered Noah Frye and his family were living in Lost River, Colorado.

"I'm sorry." Tears welled in Ruthanne's eyes. "I had no idea where a few simple comments would lead. If I'd known, I never would have mentioned a single word about any of you. You've got to believe me."

Mollie squeezed her friend's hands. "Of course, I believe you. You've never lied to me."

Noah winced. The words embedded themselves in him like fiery darts. Mollie had never lied to him, either. When he'd asked her to take care of Sam and Angela, she'd been forthright about her yearning to help her family, even when it meant her working two jobs at the same time. She was doing more than her share of the chores at the Lehman home. She'd told him she would do the job to the best of her ability, and she'd been honest.

It was his turn to be honest. It was long overdue, and he hoped it wasn't too late.

Mollie's head was spinning. She'd never guessed Ruthanne had set the wheels in motion to bring Noah's in-laws to Lost River.

As her friend turned to leave, she motioned for Mollie to *komm* with her. Ruthanne paused when Noah went into the house, as Sam came to the door asking for more *millich*.

"Forgive me?" Ruthanne asked.

"For what? You didn't do anything wrong. Not like…" She hoped the sudden heat on her face wasn't visible in the thickening twilight.

"Like Albert, you mean?"

"I'm sorry, Ruthanne. I shouldn't have mentioned him. I'm working on forgiving him."

She was astonished when Ruthanne chuckled. "I am, too. I've spent hours on my knees this week thanking God that He opened my eyes before it was too late. Things haven't been right, but I tried to ignore it, listening to my hopes of getting married. I know the only One I should listen to is God. You've forgiven me, Mollie, and you're on your way to forgiving Albert. Isn't there someone else you should be able to forgive more easily than Albert?"

"You mean Noah."

"Of course. You love him, and anyone can see he loves you and his kids do, too. It's time for you to stop thinking you don't deserve to be happy."

"I'm happy. I've got my family, my friends, my scholars."

"You're content. That's not the same thing." Without another word, Ruthanne headed along the road toward her house.

Mollie turned to her own. From the house came giggles and a deeper laugh. She ached to be a part of that family circle.

When she opened the door, two small forms rushed toward her, talking over each other and so quickly that she couldn't understand a word they were saying. Noah walked toward her, and she raised her eyes toward his. The moment their gazes connected and melded, her burden of anger and frustration thawed and fell away like icicles from the eaves at the beginning of spring after a long and difficult winter. Ruthanne had been right. Mollie had come to accept that contentment was all she deserved, but God hadn't put love into her heart so she could ignore it.

Mollie guided the *kinder* to the table and gave them another small piece of cake each, along with refilling their glasses. Only then did she return to where Noah waited.

"Are you here to say goodbye as the kids believe you are?" she asked point-blank.

He grasped her hands, drawing her a half step forward. "Before I answer, let me ask why you left the hospital the other night."

"You and your family needed time together. You didn't need an outsider there."

"Is that how you see yourself? An outsider?" One side of his mouth quirked. "None of us sees you that way. I've spent the last five years wanting family, but denying my own. I lied to myself so long I began to believe the lies." He shook his head with a rueful grin. "I never realized how easy it is to accept a lie if I repeated it often enough. That was easier than facing the truth."

She squeezed his hands. "You aren't hiding behind lies any longer."

"I thank God for that with every breath I take. I never would have described myself as a coward. In fact, I'd convinced myself I was the opposite because I took on the task of raising two young *kinder* while chasing a dream I never was grateful God brought into my life."

"He knows how much joy you receive from your work that helps others."

"He also knows how much joy I've received from having you here to help me. I don't know if I can thank you for being here as a teacher for me and for the *kinder*. *Danki*, Mollie." He gave her a heart-stopping smile, but released her hands.

She bit her lower lip, not wanting it to quiver. His thanks had sounded too much like goodbye, but she needed to be honest, too.

"*Danki* to you, Noah, for opening your family to me. Spending time with you and Angela and Sam has brought me so much happiness—happiness I wasn't sure I deserved."

"Why?"

"Because I felt I'd done something bad when I was hurt." Her fingers went to her cheek again, but he halted them, folding them between his own. "I know the truth now."

"Will you tell me someday?"

"*Ja.*" Tears weighed on her lashes as his question suggested he might return…someday. "You were right. Memories are precious, whether they're *gut* or sad."

"I hope we make many more."

"In Lost River?" She hesitated, then said, "Rumor in town is you're leaving for Pennsylvania."

"Rumor is wrong."

"It is?" she choked out past her shock. She'd been so sure he'd want to let Angela and Sam get to know their grandparents and the rest of their extended family in Lancaster County.

"I've been offered a ton of work this week. A job in California, but I'm not going to take that one. I don't need to run away like I thought I should. I need to give my kids stability while I deal with my past. Our past. I sent some dark sky ideas to the Saguache County Arts Consortium, and they quickly let me know they liked them." His grin looked as young and mischievous as his son's. "I've also been contacted about a project in Pagosa Springs and another near Aspen. There's a lot of interest in creating quilt trails."

"That's *wunderbaar.*"

"Only if I can find someone to take care of Angela and Sam while I work."

She bit back a half sob. He might not be going to Lancaster County, but he also wasn't planning on staying in

Lost River much longer. Saguache County was a huge county with a low population. A barn-quilt trail might be the perfect way to bring more people to the spread out towns, especially those who were visiting the Great Sand Dunes National Park. The county seat was more than an hour away from Lost River by car. He'd have to move there to complete his projects.

"Will you?" he asked.

"Will I what?"

Instead of replying, he cupped her chin and tilted her face toward his. As he pressed his lips over hers, it was more glorious than she'd imagined. His kiss was gentle, as if he feared she'd pull away. When she didn't, he deepened the kiss, his arms around her holding her close. Her own curved around his shoulders, delighting in the tickle of his hair against her skin.

Putting his mouth close to her ear, he whispered, "Be my wife. Marry me, Mollie."

"I can't."

"You can't?" He pulled back enough so his gaze could hold hers. "Why not?"

She explained what the *doktor* had told her after the buggy accident. "I see how you love *kinder*, Noah, and I can't give you more."

Again, he whispered against her hair, "You give me more joy than I believed possible. Please keep bringing your joy with life and your brilliant smile into my life. Into my family's lives. It'll be the perfect-size family if you'll become a part of it."

"Say *ja*, Mollie," urged Angela, throwing her uninjured arm around Mollie's waist.

"Ja, ja, ja," chanted Sam as he bounced around them with excitement.

She looked down, realizing she'd been so lost in Noah's kiss she hadn't heard the *kinder* join them. "How did you know what he asked?"

"Because it's what he should ask." Angela looked at her as if she'd lost her mind to ask such a foolish question. "And you should say *ja*."

Noah squatted so he could meet his *kinder*'s gazes. "No coercion."

"What's co-co… Whatever you said?" asked the little boy.

"It means," Noah replied, "Mollie needs to make up her mind on her own. She doesn't need input from you two."

"I do," Mollie argued. "If they don't wanted me as their…" She choked on *mamm*, a word she never had imagined would describe her. Swallowing hard, she pushed on. "If they said no, I would have listened."

Noah stood and put his arm around her. As he drew her close again, she saw nothing but his warm, dark eyes. How much they had changed from the first time she'd looked into them and saw fatigue and grief and anger at God! She'd recognized each of those emotions, because the same had consumed her. Somehow, sometime, somewhere along the way since that first evening, when he'd stood on her family's front porch with his family in tow, the burdens they carried had vanished. What they'd endured remained, but at last she believed she could move past them and into the future with hope and faith…and love. She believed, as she lost herself in his loving gaze, he could, too.

"Mollie, I'm tired of running from life. I want to run toward something. Toward you," Noah said. "You love my son and daughter, and they love you."

"You left out one important person." She framed his face. "*Ich liebe dich*, Noah Frye. I love you with all my heart."

"*Ich liebe dich*, Mollie Lehman. Will you take this peculiar journey with us through the San Luis Valley and only the *gut* Lord knows where else?" His voice dropped to a sibilant whisper. "With me? As my wife? I know I asked you before, but you never gave me an answer. Will you say *ja*?"

"Should I?" She smiled at the youngsters, whom she'd soon call her son and daughter.

"*Ja, ja, ja!*" cheered the *kinder* as they danced around her and Noah.

"That's three votes," Noah said with a smile. "Want to make it unanimous?"

Mollie grinned. "*Ja!*"

Epilogue

Two months later

The wedding had been *wunderbaar*. Everyone had celebrated sharing the bride's and groom's happiness. Young and old, each guest was delighted that Viola Lehman and Howard Zehr had become husband and wife.

"Your *mamm* hasn't stopped smiling." Noah grinned as he clasped Mollie's hand. "Will you look as happy on our wedding day?"

"You don't have long to wait and see. Our wedding is two weeks from today." She squeezed his fingers. "It was kind of you to agree to postpone it so *Mamm* and Howard could have their special day first."

"I've learned—or I'm trying to learn—the lesson you've shared with Sam and Angela over and over."

"That *gut* things *komm* to those who wait?"

"Also how we must trust those we love to be there for us, even when we don't know how to ask for their help."

She leaned her head on his shoulder and breathed in the musky scent of his soap and shampoo. They'd become her favorite fragrances. "You didn't need me to teach you that lesson, Noah. You already knew it."

In the past two months, since he'd forgiven his in-laws and himself, he'd found a way, with God's guidance, to keep his grief in balance with the rest of his life. He smiled more easily, and he'd discovered a deeper joy in his *kinder*'s company. Their response to his moments of unexpected hilarity had delighted her as much as it had Angela and Sam.

"I've got to disagree," he said with a teasing smile.

"Why am I not surprised?"

He tapped the tip of her nose playfully. "I did need your help to relearn life's important lessons. I know you'll no longer be teaching once another teacher can be found."

"It may take a few months." She'd missing being with the scholars, but the idea of taking care of her family and their home—wherever it might be—thrilled her. All her family would be nearby because Tyler wasn't leaving Lost River. At least, not yet, because he'd accepted the job at the sports-equipment store. She'd lost count of the number of times she'd thanked God for His blessings, and she wasn't done yet.

"It's going to take more than a few months for us to learn the lessons we can together."

"A lifetime."

"Sounds like the best possible plan."

As everyone shouted for the bride and groom to cut the cake, Noah took their distraction as the perfect time to steal a kiss from Mollie. She smiled into his bright eyes, knowing there would be far sweeter kisses later this evening.

She looked up as her name was called and held out her arms to enfold Sam and Angela, who'd lost two tiny teeth since the first had loosened. When Noah's arms went around all of them, she thanked God one more time.

Because this was more than contentment. This was happiness.

* * * * *

Dear Reader,

Welcome to the San Luis Valley of south-central Colorado. I was astonished when I first saw the flat fields with the Rockies on every side. Yet, at the same time I felt at home, because those fields were planted with potatoes, like where I'd grown up. With the amazing vistas, it seemed the perfect place to build a barn quilt trail to enhance the natural beauty. While Mollie Lehman has roots that go deep, Noah Frye believes he's passing through on a lifetime run from his past. But God has other plans for two hearts who have been seeking each other…though they didn't know that. Sometimes it isn't easy to see God's plans for our lives, but what joy—and often humility—there is in discovering His plans, isn't there?

Visit me at www.joannbrownbooks.com. And look for my next book coming soon!

Wishing you many blessings,
Jo Ann Brown

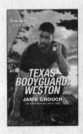

LOVE INSPIRED
INSPIRATIONAL ROMANCE

Stories to uplift and inspire

DISCOVER.

Find which books are coming next month from your favorite Love Inspired authors at
LoveInspired.com/shop/pages/new-releases.html

EXPLORE.

Sign up for the Love Inspired e-newsletter and download a free book at
TryLoveInspired.com

CONNECT.

Join our Love Inspired community to share your thoughts and connect with other readers!

f **Facebook.com/LoveInspiredBooks**

𝕏 **Twitter.com/LoveInspiredBks**

Could a temporary arrangement lead to a lifetime of happiness?

Schoolteacher Mollie Lehman loves her job, but there's one problem—her family's medical debt means she can't afford to take school breaks off. The arrival of widower Noah Frye might just be the answer she's looking for. Working as a nanny for his two children is the ideal solution...until Mollie and Noah start to fall for each other. But they've both lost too much to trust in love. Will they find the courage to face their fears and realize their perfect arrangement could also be a perfect match?

AN AMISH OF LOST RIVER NOVEL

CATEGORY: **HOPE & INSPIRATION**

$7.99 U.S./$8.99 CAN.

ISBN-13: 978-1-335-93694-3

50799

9 781335 936943

EAN

S

Uplifting stories of faith, forgiveness and hope.

LOVE INSPIRED

LoveInspired.com

LOVE INSPIRED
INSPIRATIONAL ROMANCE

A FAITHFUL
GUARDIAN

K-9 COMPANIONS

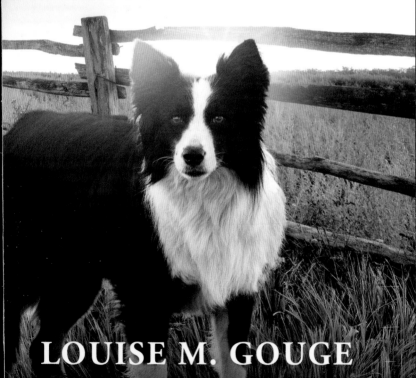

LOUISE M. GOUGE

LOVE INSPIRED
INSPIRATIONAL ROMANCE

Uplifting stories of faith, forgiveness and hope.

Fall in love with stories where faith helps guide you through life's challenges, and discover the promise of a new beginning.

Six new books available every month!